LAW
Along the Border

LAW
Along the Border

LAURAN PAINE

THORNDIKE
CHIVERS

This Large Print edition is published by Thorndike Press®, Waterville, Maine USA and by BBC Audiobooks, Ltd, Bath, England.

Published in 2004 in the U.S. by arrangement with Golden West Literary Agency.

Published in 2005 in the U.K. by arrangement with Golden West Literary Agency.

U.S. Hardcover 0-7862-7120-5 (Western)
U.K. Hardcover 1-4056-3224-0 (Chivers Large Print)
U.K. Softcover 1-4056-3225-9 (Camden Large Print)

The text of this Large Print edition is unabridged.
Other aspects of the book may vary from the original edition.

Set in 16 pt. Plantin.

Printed in the United States on permanent paper.

══

British Library Cataloguing-in-Publication Data available

══

Library of Congress Cataloging-in-Publication Data

Paine, Lauran.
    Law along the border / Lauran Paine.
      p. cm.
    ISBN 0-7862-7120-5 (lg. print : hc : alk. paper)
    1. Mexican American Border Region — Fiction.
    2. Illegal arms transfers — Fiction.   3. New Mexico —
    Fiction.   4. Large type books.   I. Title.
    PS3566.A34L39 2004
    813′.54—dc22   2004058803

LAW
Along the Border

1

PURGATORY

There was shade up where piñons and junipers grew, but otherwise the land as far as a man could see lay shimmering under midsummer sunblast, and even in among the upland tree-shelters all a man and his mount really escaped was the direct, molten yellow rays of direct sunlight. Otherwise, the shade was hot and breathless, and heavy with the peculiarly unpleasant scent of junipers.

Down in the village of Timorato where the adobe walls were three to four feet thick, it was possible to get cool.

In fact, down there were people who managed to stay cool all summer long; they operated the *cantina,* the only saloon for hundreds of miles, or they worked in one of the other fort-like old mud buildings such as the general store, the liverybarn, which had once been a barracks for Mexican soldiers, the stage company's squat, ugly office with its mud-walled corralyard out back, or they lived in one of the *jacals*, the mean little desert-dwellings which surrounded Timorato like tawny square blocks in all directions, without much evidence of planning, but Timorato was a very old town; it was said to have been created by Mexican armies back in the very early days when *Mejico* had owned all what was now the U.S. Southwest, and it was also said that Timorato, before that, had been an Indian village, which it probably had been, since Indian tools, artifacts and graves kept turning up. But all anyone actually knew now, since there had never been a written record before the priests built the church and began servicing the community with baptisms, weddings, Last Rites, was that Timorato, which was on the oldtime road up out of Mexico, was very old. What no-one had ever satisfactorily explained to the *gringos* who now owned all the south desert country, as well as the best businesses in town, was why a town was ever established there at all.

Of course there was a reason. Timorato was the first good water after one emerged up out of Mexico after making the *Jornada del Muerta*, the journey of death across the vast, waterless and desolate expanse of upper Chihuahua.

The man sitting his horse among the odorous junipers could see southward through the blue-blurred distance, down where the invisible and mostly unmarked international boundary was, and beyond, into the State of Chihuahua.

It looked all the same, on the U.S. side or the Mex side; parched, lethal, shimmering, and malevolent under midsummer's deadly pale yellow glow.

The man looked elsewhere, off in the direction of Deming, or Las Crucas, or in a more northerly direction, off towards distant Lordsburg, or even more distant Silver City. There was nothing to see but more of the same, and as the man swung to ground and stood beside his horse, he told the animal that if a man had to pick a bad place, where they now were could scarcely be improved upon. Then the man led the horse in closer, loosened the cincha, got comfortable in the heavy shade by squatting at the base of the old juniper, and settled himself for a long wait.

From a slight elevation it was usually easy to make out faint trails which a person did not notice otherwise. Perhaps because the trails leading towards Timorato were very old, even though, obviously, many of them had not been used in years, the man beneath the juniper could make them out effortlessly. It was a little like looking at a veiny kind of ghostly great spider web. The trails were there, vague and indistinct in many cases, but eerily traceable. Otherwise, there was the arrow-straight north-south roadway. It was far better maintained and showed much more usage coming from the north and ending in the town, than it showed below Timorato where it headed over the line and down into Mexico, which was probably understandable. If people intended to visit Mexico, they would go down through by way of the civilized conveniences of El Paso, lying many miles eastward, not the rude, dangerous route they would be compelled to travel reaching Timorato, and from there on down into Chihuahua, a notoriously brigand-ridden Mex province where even those agile Mexican route-armies had more or less abandoned hope of ever "pacifying" a territory so huge and waterless — and full of border-jumpers who fled up into the U.S. Territory of New Mexico, where the Mexican armies could not go, if danger threatened.

In fact, the longer the horseman squatted in hot shade with his head-hung, drowsing horse, studying this seemingly limitless expanse of purgatorial astringency, the more he marveled that anyone, even the Mexicans who were native to all this, willingly resided here, or voluntarily even visited here.

The soil was gritty with tawny sand, what grass grew at all was very sparse, very fragile, and appeared in little clumps interspersed with clumps of inedible, usually thorny, underbrush of spiny cactus, which very often sheltered a scorpion, a rattle-snake, or a great hairy black spider as large as a man's fist, who could jump faster than the eye could follow. All this, without water, and for most of the year with an unnerving, debilitating, devastating variety of heat.

The man tipped down his hat staring far out from narrowed grey eyes as he told the drowsing horse except for gold — and he doubted how much had ever come out of this land — and the few waterholes, there was not one damned single thing to recommend the south desert, and this god-forsaken border segment of it, to anyone who was in his right mind. Then the man slowly man-ufactured a cigarette, lit it, and smoked without taking his eyes off the dancing distance.

It was hot. Lizards lethargically scurried, mouths agape to pant as they did so. There were no soaring high buzzards — what the Mexicans called *sopilotes*. They did not soar this time of year after about nine in the morning. Rattlesnakes burrowed beneath cool rocks; a half hour of full exposure to that sun would kill them. And the natives of dark skin and downward-sweeping eyelashes of this land went completely somnolent between noon and nine o'clock. Even the few bands of marauding holdout-Indians who still clung to this worthless world, and who had become inured over the millennia, got sluggish during mid-day.

And yet, if a person wanted the land completely to himself, and providing he could stand the glare and heat, midday was the time to peregrinate.

That, also, the squatting man beneath the dumpy old bad-smelling juniper tree told his horse, without taking his eyes off the molten landscape spreading in all directions from Timorato.

The silence was as thick and cloying as the hush of the grave. Nothing moved.

There were eyes. Always, everywhere, there were eyes, and the squatting man knew this very well. Anything at all that was out of its element, was constantly under the surveillance of the creatures which belonged to the intruded-upon element. Without seeing them, without making any effort to locate them, the man knew he was being watched by reptile-eyes, tarantula-eyes, insect-eyes, and possibly even the eyes of the runty little foxes and coyotes who eked out a sorry existence off dehydrated carrion in this countryside.

He put out his cigarette, lifted the sweat-stained old dusty black hat to run a limp sleeve across his forehead, resettled the hat and shifted position a little, but Apache-like, he did not cease watching. Even so, it was the horse standing behind him, lower lip hanging, eyes nearly closed, who gradually roused himself, slowly lifted his head, little ears pointing onward, eyes widening under the impetus of a horse's strong curiosity, which told the man there finally was movement.

First, it appeared as little more than an odd-shaped far-away speck. Then it assumed the toy-soldier size of a horseman, and finally, the squatting man made out some of the dominant details of the rider coming on an angling course up-country, and inland, actually traveling north-easterly in the direction of the north roadway above Timorato, coming from what the squatting man assumed had been a more distant crossing from up out of Chihuahua.

The rider was not heading for the village, he was angling far out and around it in such a way that he managed to keep several miles of that dusty, brushy, gritty purgatorial landscape between himself and the town, while aiming to strike the stageroad above Timorato several miles.

The squatting man watched, occasionally swinging his head from side to side as though he expected to see other converging horsemen, but there was no other visible movement. Even down in the town there was nothing to watch, so the squatting horseman finally rose up to his full lean height and fished in his pocket for a polished oblong piece of steel which he held loosely, until he saw that distant rider dip down to cross through a shallow arroyo, then he stepped away from the juniper, raised the steel to catch sunlight, and flashed a brilliant beam once, then once again, and as the horseman emerged from the arroyo, the watcher pocketed his piece of polished metal and moved back into shade again.

He looked at his pocket-watch, canted his head at the position of the sun, turned and made a slow, careful study of all the land behind him, then tugged up his cincha and mounted the interested horse to rein away, out into the open and head down the back-side of his slight eminence where he was concealed from view until, somewhat later, he came round the tapering berm of ancient hillock to emerge upon the flat plain.

He rode westerly to cut off the retreat of that other horseman, and only occasionally glanced up where the other rider was still making his slow way in the direction of the stageroad.

Once, when an irritable rattler buzzed from its meager shade beneath a buckbrush plant, he yielded to avoid the unnecessary confrontation, and with sweat darkening his shirt as well as the sleek, dark hide of his horse, continued to scout the westerly country until, eventually, he found the sign of that other horseman, and halted to study it.

The man had crossed up out of Mexico about four miles south-westerly, out where there was no chance of his having been seen. But what interested the lean man was that there were only one set of tracks. He had expected more, at least two sets, and possibly even three or four sets, but it was that much better, if there had been only one rider crossing the border.

Now, finally, he turned and followed the

15

traces left by that other horseman, but without increasing his pace at all. This was the time of year, and the time of day, when any kind of pursuit on the south desert was undertaken at a walk. A chase under these circumstances became a macabre marathon of endurance between man and man, horse and horse, and the first one to panic and push for speed, lost.

The sun seemed not to move at all. It hung up there, skewered against a faded, pale sky full of ancient dust and crushing heat. No man in his right mind rode out like this, unless his reasons were equal to the peril he endured in a place where death in hundreds of different disguises lay on all sides.

But if a man *did* ride out, he was most likely to endure if he were, like the pursuing rider, leaned down to rawhide toughness, and imbued with the kind of self-reliance, the kind of total confidence, this grey-eyed pursuer possessed.

2

THE SPRUNG TRAP

What followed was very simple. It was also very dangerous. The man coming up-country upon the trail of that earlier, solitary horseman, went out and around exactly as the man in front of him had done. He dipped down into, and emerged upon the far side of, each of the insignificant little arroyos. He sashayed farther westerly when the tracks turned off in that direction, and for an hour he did not deviate one bit, but when he finally knew he was heading for the stageroad, which he could not yet see, through the haze and underbrush, he finally halted, sat perfectly still, and listened.

He seemed entirely alone, out there. The heat bore down, the gelatin-like dancing layers of haze obscured everything in the distance, and a mile ahead where the stageroad lay, the only sound which ultimately carried back that far, was the cry of a mating quail.

That was when the man swung down,

tied his horse and pulled forth the booted carbine before turning to walk ahead very carefully and prudently.

When he came within sight of the roadway and could look north and south, all he saw was the distant scatter of adobe buildings down where Timorato lay, far southward. Then a man's sharp voice spoke ahead, where some low old scalding-hot, corpse-colored scaly rocks stood.

"If you move I'll kill you . . . . Put your hands straight out in front and hold them there."

Where the lean man was standing, there was still nothing to see, so he angled a little, to his left, which was northward, and got closer to the road, closer to those scaly old rocks. Finally, then, he saw the back of a squatty, sweat-streaked man facing the road, a Winchester lying across the top of the nearest flat rock, both his arms rigidly pointing out front. The lean man waited a moment, then said, *"Muera,"* and the rigid man's head jerked as words tumbled in un-grammatical Spanish from his lips. He cried for his life, inspired to this by what the lean pursuer had said, which was 'may he die'.

Another man arose from the under-brush, looked over and winked at the lean pursuer, then he sauntered over, tossed the carbine to the ground, tossed down the Mexican's holstered sixgun, and lay a cool pistol-barrel against the Mexican's neck as he ordered the man to divest himself of his other weapons.

The Mexican yanked loose a boot-knife and pitched that over with the other weapons. Then he delved inside his soiled, sweaty shirt and flung down a little under-and-over derringer, and finally he turned, his mahogany features graying under layers of sweat, and, seeing his captors were *gringos*, spoke to them in their own language.

"I was traveling. I have a sister in Las Crucas. I was traveling up there."

The hawk-faced man who was closest, said, "Sure you were. Your sister up in Las Crucas is sick, and you were going up to be with her, and to help with the family."

The Mexican momentarily beamed. *"Si*, that is it exactly, *comita."*

The lean pursuer walked over, looked at the small arsenal, then raised his sardonic eyes. "And the only reason you stopped at this particular spot, hid your horse back yonder, then took up a position beside the stageroad, with your carbine atop the rock, was because that is how you always rest when you travel, and it has nothing to do

19

with the fact that the stage from Lordsburg is due past, on its run down to Timorato."

The Mexican turned, studied the bronzed features, the narrowed grey eyes, and the carbine in the lean man's hands, then slowly lowered his hands and stood in dejection, saying nothing.

The lean pursuer turned away. "Where did he hide the horse, Mack?"

His *gringo* friend jutted a square jaw. "Yonder, in some mesquite. Where did you first pick him up?"

"About a couple of miles north of the line, when he started angling around north-easterly from Timorato." The lean man glanced indifferently at their captive. "There should have been more than just him."

The hawkish man cast a far look out and around, then said, "The hell with it. Let's get him back down to town. I'm as dry as a peyote bean." Then he said, "Charley, there's a letter for us down at the company office. Handleman called out to me as I was riding out, but I didn't go back for it."

The lean man, Charley Durant, was un-interested, even though he had not re-ceived a letter in two years, and had no reason to ever expect to receive one. At least not a *personal* one. He leaned to gather the *bandido*'s armament, then turned with a grunt to prod their prisoner along.

The Mexican's horse was a sorry, abused, half-starved runty beast. From a distance Charley could not have told that, but now, looking at the animal, his feelings against its owner firmed up into a less impersonal dislike. Charley Durant was a family-less man, and he was also a good stockman; that kind of a combination usually resulted in a man having more compassion for animals than people.

When Douglas McGregor untied the sad little beast and handed over the reins to · their prisoner, Charley said, "How long have you owned that horse, *bandido?*"

The Mexican turned black eyes contemptuously. "This *caballo, Señor?* A year, I think."

Charley said, "Walk, *bandido*. Walk, and lead your horse," then he turned to go after his own animal, and when the astonished Mexican looked back where McGregor was already astride, Mack smiled. "You heard."

The Mexican flung his arms wide. "But why, *Señor?* It is four or five miles to Timorato, and the sun is bad, up there."

Mack mopped sweat with a red bandanna,

eyed the pathetic battered Mexican horse, and guessed what had annoyed his partner at this manhunting game. "You eat good, from the looks of you, Pancho. The horse doesn't look very good." Mack jerked his head. "Out to the road, turn south, and walk."

The highwayman obeyed. He was a very dark, very coarse-featured, pock-marked man with muddy eye-whites and a sour scent of stale sweat and garlic. He was, in a sense, typical of the border-jumpers who happened to also be Mexicans. He was deadly in a treacherous way, but when unarmed and captured, like he now was, there was no more obedient, deferential, almost likeable, human being alive.

When Charley Durant rode up, McGregor offered a canteen. Durant refused. He had not drunk since shortly after sunup, when he'd got up there by the juniper to start his vigil, and if he did not drink now, until he was back in Timorato, he would not have to drink again — and again.

McGregor, who was a reddish-faced man with heavy brows and a slightly hawkish cast to his strong features, drank, slung the canteen back where he usually carried it, on the right side of his saddle-swells, and rolled a cigarette as they plodded along behind their prisoner. When McGregor had the cigarette lighted, had automatically stood in his stirrups looking in all directions, he settled back saying, "The pay on this one won't be worth it, Charley. It must be a hundred and fifteen out here. I melted off five pounds back there, lying under the sagebrush waiting for this pepperbelly. Not only that, but a damned scorpion almost got me."

Charley grinned. "He'd have died."

Timorato seemed to be floating a foot off the ground, down the road a mile or so. It shimmered and danced and appeared to rise and fall slightly, above the ground.

McGregor called ahead to the copiously perspiring border-jumper. "Hey, *pistolero,* what does Timorato mean?"

The Mexican paused and looked back. As he replied he flung off excess sweat, then dragged a filthy sleeve across his face for what sweat remained. "It means someone who is full of the fear of God, *Señor.*"

McGregor digested this and wryly shook his head. He motioned for the Mexican to resume walking, and as this was done, Mack turned and said, "They always give their landmarks names like that. Sangre de Cristo, for instance, the blood of Christ, or

Pueblo de los Angeles, town of the angels." He turned back to studying the rude little mud village on ahead. "Full of the fear of God. . . ."

Charley smiled. "If I had to live there, Mack, maybe I'd have that kind of fear. Look at it, stuck out in the middle of nowhere, with Indians and Mex marauders and *gringo* renegades hitting it whenever they damned well feel like it. Look at Pancho, there; what the hell could he have got off the stage? Maybe twenty, thirty dollars, and for that he'd risk his greasy hide. Fear of God isn't too wrong; it's a lousy land any way you look at it."

McGregor finished his smoke, broke it atop the saddlehorn and pitched it aside. Charley Durant was right. Maybe not about that fear of God business, but about the rest of it. It was a mean, deadly place, peril existed in every direction; what men did not scheme to do in the way of violence and cruelty, nature accomplished.

By the time they reached the outskirts of Timorato, and encountered a bent old burnt-black Mexican faggot-gatherer with his sad-faced little stolid burro, neither one of whom had more than a half dozen teeth, it was possible to put it all in a kind of perspective; the heat, the maddening sameness of the landscape for farther than a man could ride in ten days, the grinding poverty of the people, the ugliness of life down here, and its hopelessness.

Unless a person managed that, figured a way to put it in perspective, he either could not remain, or, if he *did* remain, he gradually went crazy. There had been a lot of crazy men on the south desert; people recognized them, gauged their degrees of insanity, and avoided them as best they could.

There were never very many crazy natives, neither Indians nor Mexicans. The Indians were highly mobile, which they had to be in order to survive at all, and the Mexicans were not so much apathetic, which was how most *gringos* thought of them, as they were basically and inherently fatalistic. They had very few principles and fewer ethics. Their south-desert world was not a place where people could afford the luxury of either. Survival mattered and nothing else. A *Señor Quijote* could not have lasted on the south desert one month.

McGregor and Durant were not natives; at least they had not been born in the Southwest, but both had spent much of their lives down there, but usually in a less hostile and impoverished area than they were now in. But that could change, and in fact it *had* changed, almost monthly ever since they had quit as gunguards on the bullion runs, to accept employment as special agents.

Wherever company losses were exorbitant as a result of robbery, McGregor and Durant appeared. This rarely endeared them to local peace officers, a matter which did not much worry either of them, and it also had kept them riding back and forth the full distance of the Mex–U.S. border country year in and year out. They were well known. Not always well-liked, but quite well known.

Their pay was not magnanimous. In fact, it was less, as special agents, than it had been as bullion gunguards — the highest paid of company employees because the mortality rate was also very high — but McGregor and Durant had become adequately professional at their work to actually make more. They were not forbidden by the company, or the law, from claiming head-money, and the company helped in this regard by promptly offering healthy rewards.

Except that, in this particular instance, they did not seem to have anything but another hungry, solitary, coach-hunter. If there was a reward on him, it probably only existed in Mexico, where McGregor

26

and Durant seldom went, except in hot pursuit, and where they were not welcome. Neither could they collect bounties down there; the Mexicans were not pleased when *gringo* manhunters ran down bandits in their territory. They always adopted an attitude that it was unsportsmanlike for *gringos* to do that in Mexico. In fact, they had a custom, down there, of shooting men like McGregor and Durant on sight.

Their captive, this time, dressed poorly, and except for the quality of his guns, was an unlikely prospect. Still, there was the primary consideration, which was to nail highwaymen, and while it may have been disgruntling to some manhunters to have spent a dehydrating day catching an outlaw who was not going to add anything to their bank accounts, neither McGregor nor Durant were that mercenary.

They were, in fact, that most deadly of manhunters, men who had chosen their calling and who still followed it, not for any very lofty idealistic reasons, but because neither of them could abide a liar nor a thief. It was a fairly simple philosophy, but neither Douglas McGregor nor Charles Durant were very complicated men. They were vastly experienced, competitively capable, and had no use for outlaws.

3

ONE UNWASHED BANDIDO

The law in Timorato was administered by a Texan whose angular build and curly dark hair made him seem to be very alien among the mostly *mestizo* populace, who were usually much shorter, thicker, and with perfectly straight hair.

His name was James Corbett, but he was called "Cap", as a result of having been a Confederate officer during the Rebellion. When he accepted the sore-footed Mexican *bandido* from Durant and McGregor, he hardly more than glanced at the new prisoner; he'd been holding men like that for more than ten years, in his massive old adobe *calabozo*, and was far more interested in the pair of strangers who had brought him in, and who now showed him their papers of authority from the Southwest Stage & Cartage Company.

His first question was: "How's come you boys didn't come to see me first?"

Durant gave a dry answer. "Marshal, when you first arrive in a strange country, you just naturally don't know who your friends are."

The Texan made an expansive gesture. "Hell, boys," he exclaimed, "folks down here are on the side of law and order every time. Now you take that greaser you brought in — if I wanted to hang him out back on the scaffold, folks would favor it, even the Messican folks." He gestured. "He'p yourself to coffee, yonder on the stove, while I lock this feller up. Then we'll set down and talk a little."

After the town marshal had disappeared down a gloomy corridor, herding the Mexican ahead of him, McGregor put a skeptical stare upon his partner. "Even if he wasn't a Texan, I'd be wary of him. I just never trusted the ones that started bending over backwards, first off."

Durant went for the coffee, which was bad and black, and very bitter, without commenting. When the marshal returned, though, he said, "I had an idea Arch Handleman at the stage office might have told you we'd arrived, Marshal. We rode in late last night and bedded down at his corralyard."

The Texan stepped behind his littered,

unkempt desk and sat down, smiling. "Well, boys, I got to tell you — me 'n old Arch don't just see to an eye some of the time."

McGregor went after some of the coffee, too, but after one swallow he gently put aside the cup and stepped to a wall-bench to sit, and go to work rolling a smoke.

"If there's a reward," he said casually, "we'll put in for it." He lit up, watched the marshal's face a moment, through smoke, then smiled across the room. "It probably won't be much, though. And there is a runty little Mex horse. . . ."

"Aw hell," exclaimed the Texan, "keep him. He'p yourself to the horse for your bother. Now tell me something; how's come you fellers to be here at all? Timorato don't get much stage trade, and in all the years I been down here, I've never seen a single bullion coach come through." Marshal Corbett's dark, bright-hard eyes lingered on McGregor. "In fact, the coach which was supposed to arrive this morning, didn't even show up."

Durant said, "The reason for that, Marshal, is because Mack and I sent back word for it not to show up, once we heard a rumor down over the line in a *cantina,* someone was going to stop it."

Corbett's amiability covered this small surprise capably. He smiled and leaned back in his chair. "I declare; you boys got influence with the company, then." He let that compliment lie, before saying, "But what was aboard, that Southwest sent you lads on ahead? Not bullion; I never seen any bullion come through, in all the years I been here."

Durant finished the coffee and dunked the cup in a bucket of water before hanging the cup upon one of the nails in the wall, beside other hanging cups. "The only thing that was aboard that particular stage, Marshal, was a coffin, and I expect the mail sacks."

The Texan acted mildly derisive. "Couldn't have been the mail, drew that greaser up over the line. We never got a *full* mail sack since I been the law down here. Even the letters that *do* come in, don't have no money in them."

Durant was not particularly interested, and after spending as much time along the Texas–Mexican border as he had, the past few years, he was a little skeptical of Texans, therefore when next he spoke, whether the Texan detected the faint drag of speech, denoting distaste, McGregor detected it. But McGregor had been with

31

Durant those years down along the Mexican line in Texas, and understood this change in his partner's mood as well as he had understood it back up where they'd caught that *bandido.*

When Durant said, "If it wasn't the mail pouch, it must have been the coffin," McGregor had to concentrate on not laughing at the look on Marshal Corbett's raffish face.

The lawman said, "Coffin? You said the coffin, didn't you, Mister Durant? Now what in gawd's name would even a Messican want with a coffin?"

"This coffin had a Mexican in it. I don't know what his name was. I saw it on a manifest up in Lordsburg, but don't remember it now. Anyway, I think if you bring Pancho back out here, and make a point out of getting him to talk to you, Marshal, I think he'll say he was after the coffin."

Jim Corbett just could not quite accept this. "That don't make one lick of sense, boys. I can't rightly imagine anyone wantin' an *empty* coffin, but sure not a *full* one."

Durant gazed out a recessed, barred front window into the roadway. The sun was still lying in wait out there. It did not appear to have moved one iota since the pair of stage company men had entered the jailhouse.

Durant did not respond to the Texan's questions, so Douglas McGregor did, he said, "Ask the prisoner, Marshal. I'd guess maybe he knew the man in the box; maybe he was even going to take him off with him." McGregor thought about that, then scowled. "Not on *that* horse, he wasn't." Then McGregor arose, cigarette hanging, thumbs hooked in his shellbelt, gazing over at the angular, long-legged Texan.

Mack was not a tall man. That is, he had never achieved six feet in height, although he was only a couple of inches under it, and his breadth, his obvious physical strength, more than made up the difference. Mack feared nothing that rode or walked or slithered. Now, he turned towards the door and waited there until Durant joined him, then he said, "Marshal, if you find out that Mexican is worth anything, we'd take it kindly if you let us know." Then McGregor opened the door.

The heat came up like a solid substance and struck with breathtaking scorch as soon as people left the cool, usually gloomy, interior of one of those ancient mud buildings. It did this now, as

McGregor and Durant lingered a moment beneath the jailhouse overhang before stepping forth into roadway dust heading for the *cantina.*

They seemed to be almost phlegmatic men, at times, the way they bored right ahead into this unpleasant heat, and as they had upon other occasions, in the past, done the same thing in the face of trouble.

The saloonman was crippled. Not altogether noticeably, but when he walked one side of his body made a fluid stoop, straightened up, then stooped again. Whatever it was that inhibited his natural movement, was not visible to someone across the bar from him.

He was a thin-lipped man with grey at the temples, who nevertheless did not actually seem that old. When he brought down a bottle and two glasses, set them up and made a barman's quick, wise assessment, he said, "It was just a gamble." He smiled. "When fellers come through the door I try and figure whether they're whisky or tequila or beer drinkers."

Durant smiled back. "You make any bets with yourself?"

"Sure. Always." The barman shifted his weight with noticeable effort and pointed to a glass jar upon the backbar. It was about half full of copper pennies. "When it's full I give it to the priests." He leaned forward, dragging his injured leg around. "That's when I lose." His eyes twinkled genially. "Well, gents . . . ?"

McGregor answered. "No penny for the priest, *amigo*. We're whisky men."

The barman hitched around and limped off, up towards the north end of the bar where three sun-blasted *vaqueros* were sipping glass-clear tequila. Every one of them had ivory grips on his sixgun, but they did not wear the large sombreros or the tight-fitting, embroidered trousers of Mexican cowboys — *vaqueros*.

Durant leaned down to relax and watch McGregor fill their glasses. He eyed that jar of copper pennies and said, "Hell; I'd guess the priests don't do too well in here."

Mack did not comment, he hoisted the whisky and dropped it straight down, then he made a grimace. "Green as a gourd," he said. "Next time I'll take tequila. At least *that* can't be bad. Tequila is *always* terrible. You expect that."

He turned, glancing over his shoulder as a stocky, perspiring man wearing a green eyeshade pushed in out of the sunblast, and murmured, "Handleman," as he faced fully forward again.

35

The stocky man walked over, leaned solidly against the bar, then said, "I thought you'd let me know that you caught one."

McGregor, who was closest, answered tactfully. "We were going to come over and let you know as soon as we got through in here." He turned his square, rugged, reddish face. "He wasn't worth the effort, anyway."

Handleman leaned and scowled darkly. "No? Well, I seen him. The marshal showed him to me. He was worth the effort all right."

Both the manhunters grew interested. Durant even called for another glass and when it arrived, poured it full for the stage company's local manager. As Durant shoved the glass around Mack to Handleman, he said, "You know him? Is he worth anything?"

Handleman's thick face closed down in concentration until he had downed the whisky, then, instead of promptly replying to Durant's questions, he made a terrible face and announced in ringing tones that this was without any possible question, the worst gawd-damned whisky he had ever drunk in his life. Then, with the limping bar-owner glaring down at him, he lowered his voice and said, "That greaser's name is Alfredo Montenegro. He used to ride with

36

the *jefe* they called the Panther of Chihuahua. When the *Rurales* caught the Panther with his back to a steep mountain, and cut him to pieces, Montenegro and about two dozen men escaped. They turned into a band of marauders. Last year someone caught them raiding a mine over in Arizona, and the last I heard there was only about a dozen of them left."

Handleman, having delivered this vignette, settled upon the bartop looking pleased with himself. McGregor, whose eyes had never left the older, thicker man's face, now made his comment. "That's very interesting. Wouldn't you say that was very interesting, Charley?"

Durant gravely nodded his head.

"But," said McGregor, "Mister Montenegro's history doesn't mean a damned thing to us, Mister Handleman — unless you happen to know he's also worth a bounty on this side of the line."

Arch Handleman looked steadily at the pair of manhunters. "I don't think there's a dime on him up here. In fact, Jim Corbett was searching through his stacks of wanted dodgers when I entered his office a while back, and he said he could not find a single damned thing on anyone named Alfredo Montenegro. . . . But . . . I happen to know

37

from some of the Mex hostlers I keep over at the corralyard, that Alfredo Montenegro is a damned important man down over the line, around Las Casitas."

Durant sighed, considered the whisky bottle, and evidently decided against another shot because he pushed the glass from in front of him, and leaned down with both arms hooked over the bar, as he said, "Mister Handleman; down around Las Casitas this particular pepperbelly may be a big pumpkin. Up here, with no bounty on him, he just smells of garlic and sweat, and that's about the size of it."

McGregor faintly frowned as he stood eyeing the stage company's manager. "Mister Handleman, would you say that if Montenegro rode all the way up here from Las Casitas, and kept right on riding out and around your town to stop a stage, which he obviously had to know was due, and which Charley and I had heard was going to be stopped up there . . . would you say Montenegro had to also know what was on that stage?"

Arch Handleman nodded without any hesitation. "He knew. You can bet your last *peso* that he knew." Handleman reached inside his shirt, pulled forth a limp envelope and dropped it in front of McGregor.

"This here is the letter I yelled at you about when you was riding out before sunup this morning. I got one pretty much like it. In fact, in *my* letter, it states in plain English what's in *your* letter. Read it, gents, and you'll see damned well that Montenegro knew what was on the coach. *Then* I'll tell you something else about Alfredo Montenegro." Handleman pointed, "Go ahead, open the envelope and read."

McGregor picked up the envelope.

4

A FRESH ASSIGNMENT

Geography was the catalyst which formed the environment of a country, and which also sustained, as well as formed, the people in that country. Mexico, even in its richest regions, was not a wealthy nation, but out upon its vast arid wastes, impoverishment reached beyond the thin and undernourished soil to mould the soul and spirit of the people. Occasionally, someone with wealth accumulated hundreds of miles of this desert wasteland and ran cattle upon it. In this way, even such a poor land was compelled to grudgingly sustain wealth. But it took many hundreds of square miles of land to do this, and even then it could not be done unless all the cattle and horses — and people — who resided on the desert were squeezed down to a bare-bones existence, in order that one family could live well.

From this kind of a situation had traditionally come Mexico's ragged armies and her most influential *pronunciados,* the lean, dark, vulture-like individuals riding silvered saddles, who mustered *peon* armies of the hopeless and the toil-worn, as they made their terrible revolutions, their pronouncements against the Central Government.

Most men who had spent much time on the south desert understood this; maybe they did not fully understand *why* it happened this way, but they certainly knew from observation, if from nothing else, that this was the country where the straggling great drunken hordes of ragged peons came from, and they knew the kind of demagogues who mustered them, then led them across the blood-slippery belly of their native land, leaving in their wake devastation and horror on a miles-wide scale.

They also knew something else. The letter McGregor read, then handed to Durant, specifically spelled it out. The arms for Mexican insurrections did not originate in Mexico, where ignorance as well as disinclination, kept anyone from very successfully manufacturing anything requiring the skill and patience that went into making guns.

A trickle of weapons came from Europe, but since Mexico never had adequate funds, and European weapons-merchants, having learned painfully how indifferent Mexicans were about paying debts, only sold for cash on the barrel head, therefore there was never enough guns from overseas, which left the American suppliers up over the border, to fill this void. They did it.

Who financed this trade? There was no easy answer and never had been, but *someone* paid. It was rumored that the English put up the money in order to accomplish a penetration of Mexico's mining opportunities; an occasional exposé proved there was some reason to believe this. But it was also said that American interests, for a variety of reasons, also footed the bill. But this was a question for someone else to resolve, all McGregor and Durant knew, after reading their letter from Southwest's main office, over in El Paso, was that a Mexican known as the Lion of Coahuila, was preparing to pronounce, and the dead Mexican in his wooden coffin being sent to Timorato for burial, was bringing the message the Lion of Coahuila awaited, stating that the funding for armaments had been arranged for in the U.S., and that the weapons would shortly be sent down through Texas by wagon. The executives of

Southwest Stage & Cartage Company also informed Durant and McGregor, that the Pinkerton Detective Agency, hired by the U.S. government, was vigorously tracing back to find the originator of that message, so that the government could stop this traffic before it got started, and Southwest wanted McGregor and Durant to learn everything they could, at the Timorato end.

Arch Handleman, sipping whisky while his younger companions read their letter, and pondered its contents, eventually said, "The message to Mister What's-his-name down in Coahuila, was in the pocket of the dead Mex in the coffin. Very clever. And Montenegro wasn't going to rob the coach, nor haul off the coffin, he was simply going to open it and take the message off the dead man."

McGregor nodded. He had wondered what Montenegro's purpose was. He had wondered how, exactly, Montenegro expected to take the coffin away on that miserable little half-starved horse. Now he knew the answers, but something else began to trouble him, so he said, "Mister Handleman; this isn't the same as running down highwaymen. Why the hell don't they just send along the army?"

Handleman had no answer, although he

certainly had an opinion. "Who knows? I'd guess they don't want this Lion of Coahuila gent to know he's being scuttled."

"Or," put in Charley Durant thoughtfully, "they don't give a damn about the Lion of Coahuila, they want to find out who is backing him, up here in the U.S., and if there's a big ruckus, his backer is going to go into hiding."

Handleman accepted this suggestion. "Something like that, maybe. The point is — those people down in Mexico'll know something is wrong when Montenegro don't return, with his damned message."

McGregor changed his mind, refilled the glass, also refilled Charley Durant's glass, then shoved the bottle towards Handleman as he said, "And just where do Charley and I come out, on this mess? Who pays, Mister Handleman?"

The stage-company manager did not know. "All my letter said, aside from repeating what's in your letter, is that I'm to support you fellers every way that I can." Handleman saw McGregor's head come around, slowly, and spoke quickly, again. "That don't mean with money. Nothing was said in my letter about giving you boys any money. I don't have it to give you anyway." Handleman, darkly scowling,

44

concentrated on pouring, then he pulled forth a big blue bandanna and mopped his face and neck. "It's a lousy mess," he exclaimed. "What the hell. . . . If Montenegro gets back to Chihuahua and tells 'em down there you fellers grabbed him before he could raid my coach, they'll be suspicious. Why in the hell didn't you just let him stop the stage?"

Neither Durant nor McGregor answered Handleman's question. They both drank their whisky, exchanged a look, then nodded to the stage-company's local headman, and walked out of the saloon.

Handleman turned to watch their exit, brows down in unhappy bewilderment. A voice behind him said, "Arch; that'll be fifty cents," and Handleman turned back, facing the saloonman. He looked at the two empty glasses where Durant and McGregor had been standing, at the two-thirds empty bottle, then he groaned aloud and dug in a pocket. "They roped me in," he told the saloonman. "Bob, those two fellers roped me in slick as a whistle."

The saloonman was not very sympathetic. He waited until his money had been deposited upon the bartop, then asked a question. "Who are they, Arch?"

"Couple of Southwest's special agents."

The saloonman's eyes widened slightly. "Stage company bounty hunters?"

Handleman shied away from accepting that definition. "Not *bounty* hunters, exactly, Bob. More like — well — sort of like Texas Rangers, or U.S. Marshals, only they work for Southwest."

"Here, in Timorato?"

Handleman saw that he was getting in deeper than he liked, so he said, "Passing through, more than likely. I don't have no authority over them. They work directly out of the head office over at El Paso."

The saloonman counted his money, then palmed it as he looked thoughtfully in the direction of his roadway door. "Arch, when bounty hunters ride into Timorato, they aren't just riding through," he said, and slowly turned his gaze back to Handleman, who bristled slightly, because what Bob Grant had just said amounted to a contradiction to what *he* had said.

Handleman turned acidy. "No? What the hell is there in this lousy place that would interest men like McGregor and Durant?"

Bob Grant lifted thin shoulders, and let them drop. "*You* tell *me*. . . . If I was to guess, I'd say they're after either some border-jumpers from Chihuahua, or some outlaws coming down from up north trying to reach Mexico." The saloonman's blue eyes lingered speculatively upon Arch Handleman. "Who else do we get, in this damned country, Arch?"

Handleman, who had known Bob Grant quite a few years, leaned over and said softly, "You know the answer to the question of livin' a long time, Bob?"

Grant, prematurely grey, a quiet man with reason to be quiet, slowly inclined his head. "I'm talking to *you*," he answered. "Is there anything wrong with that?"

Handleman, having made his point, loosened where he was leaning and softly sighed. "No; nothing wrong in that at all. But it had ought to stay like that."

Grant picked up the two-thirds empty bottle of whisky, nodded to Handleman, and turned away.

Arch lingered a moment longer at the bar, beginning to feel troubled and harassed. Life in Timorato was not as bad as most people thought it had to be; at least it wasn't when a man had a decent wage coming in regularly, and had a position of trust and responsibility. But — the south desert was exactly what Bob Grant had implied that it was. A highway for fleeing outlaws from the north, and marauding *pistoleros* from the south, with Timorato in the middle, and a man had to be good at balancing upon the knife's edge even under normal circumstances. . . . And now *this*, for Chriz'sake!

Handleman went back outside, let the doors of the saloon swing-to behind him, and paused as everyone always did when they emerged from a cool interior to the blast-furnace fury of the midsummer roadway, to squinch up his eyes. Two men, one on each side of the doorway, turned to accompany Arch across to his shady, gloomy company office. He looked, groaned to himself, and started forward as he said, "Damn it all, fellers, why don't you just manage this affair in your own way, and leave me out of it."

Durant's lean features were grave as he quietly said, "Mister Handleman, the letter from El Paso said you were to lend us your support."

They reached the far side of the dusty roadway, moved into the shade over there, and as Arch Handleman pushed into his office with Durant and McGregor following after, he turned and said, "I don't know what I can do for you, and that's an honest fact. I got a few spare horses out in the yard, and some extra guns, but hell,

48

even my hostlers are Messicans, and in this kind of a mess you dasn't rely on any greaser. So what could I possibly — ?"

"How well do you know Marshal Corbett?" asked McGregor, standing easy, thumbs hooked in his gunbelt, regarding the older and squatter man.

"Know him?" exclaimed Handleman. "Well; we been friends a few years. Why?"

"Because," stated Durant, "neither Mack nor I can go down there and arrange for Montenegro's release. That wouldn't fool anyone, not even Montenegro, would it? But — *you* could do that, Mister Handleman. Montenegro must realize there is someone in the country hereabouts who is working with his revolutionary people. . . . You take care of that for us, and we'll get word back to El Paso to let the coffin come along on the next coach, and after that, you probably won't see either Mack or me again. Unless, maybe, we come through Timorato some time later, in pine boxes."

Handleman threw up short, powerful arms. "What the hell do you think I am? I can't just go down and tell Cap Corbett to let that greaser loose. I'm only the feller who runs the —"

"Mister Handleman," said Douglas

McGregor. "If you don't help us just this much, we're going to have to move in here and set up our headquarters in your office, while we're trying to get to the bottom of this lousy mess. That might take all summer. It also might stir up a lot of local Mexicans . . . who shoot at people in the dark."

Handleman dropped his arms, sank down behind a battered old table which served as a desk, and stared at the pair of sun-darkened, rawhide-tough men in front of him. "It will take one hundred dollars," he said, very quietly. "All I got in the drawer right now, is sixty dollars."

McGregor began to scowl. He was not a man who voluntarily parted with money, ever, except in very small amounts over a bar or in a poker session, but he was not even very good at that.

Durant's expression did not change as he dug into a trouser pocket, counted out forty dollars from a sweat-flattened packet of notes, and tossed them upon the tabletop. As he put back the remainder of his money he looked sardonically at Handleman. "Nice lawman you got. Well; at least he don't sell out cheap." Durant stepped back towards the door. "Whisper to Montenegro that the coffin will be on the dawn stage day after tomorrow. And one more thing — don't let him take that little half-starved, beat-down horse of his. Give him a mule out of your corral. Make it a mean one. All right?"

Handleman did not question any of this. He was too relieved to have this visit terminate. The only thing he said, as he arose and picked up the greenbacks, was: "Remember now; you said this was all I'd have to do for you fellers."

5

A COTTONWOOD SPRING

North of Timorato on the Las Crucas road was the horse ranch of a man named Dalton who, it was rumored, had once been a Missouri redleg, one of those hard-riding men of pro-slavery persuasion who had, before and during the U.S. Civil War, raided over into Abolitionist Kansas shooting and burning and killing.

Dalton had not been a young man in many years, but this showed mostly in his face, which was as lined and seamed and scored as the time-ravaged south desert itself. Otherwise, though, he was thin and sinewy, tough and agile and ageless. He also owned six sections of slightly better range than existed down around Timorato, where he raised good horses.

He was a single man. If he'd ever had a family no one in the Territory had ever heard of it. He was also very handy with weapons, so when he rode upon two men lolling in camp at one of his tree-shaded water-holes, he left his horse behind a landswell, stalked the loafers on foot, and when Durant caught slight movement from the corner of his eyes and rolled to his feet gun in hand, old Dalton dropped like stone, pushed ahead his Winchester and said, "Don't cock that pistol, mister."

McGregor, half asleep, had not seen Charley arise and had no idea there was another soul within a hundred miles until he heard that gruff command. He opened both eyes, looked around, caught sunlight's reflection of blue steel, and turned to stone, staring.

Durant did not cock his sixgun, but neither did he remove his thumb from the hammer nor take his eyes off the vague silhouette of a lanky, thin man behind a clump of dusty sage.

McGregor, waiting for whatever happened next, finally spoke. "Well; do *something,* mister," and the carbine-barrel shifted a hair's-breadth to also include Mack in its range.

"Put up your gun," Dalton commanded.

Charley Durant obeyed, then waited until the man behind the bush arose, Winchester held low in both hands, to make a hostile examination of the pair of younger men. He looked longest at their horses, which were sleek, work-hardened, well-cared-for beasts. Finally, as he started towards the water-hole camp he said, "For horse thieves, you're not going to better yourselves on my range. I got damned few animals as good as the ones you're riding now."

Charley answered shortly. "We're not horse thieves. There wasn't any sign saying folks couldn't stop over at this waterhole."

Dalton halted in tree-shade, lowered his gun-barrel a little and made a closer inspection of the pair of special agents. "Who are you?" he demanded. "What you doing here?"

McGregor sat up, shoved back his hat, and vigorously scratched as he answered. "Just a couple of fellers passing through. We figured to lie over a day or so at this spring. Damned few trees in this country and even less running water." He considered Dalton. "You own this range?"

Dalton nodded. "Yeah. Six square miles of it, and it's just a little bit better than the southward land, but nowhere nearly as good as the northward land."

McGregor smiled a little. The older man had spoken the truth about his land. He said, "Care for some coffee?" and motioned towards the little dented pot upon some stones where coals glowed.

Dalton walked up still closer, leaned upon his Winchester and shook his head. "I et two hours ago." He glanced again at the nearby hobbled horses, standing hip-shot, full as ticks of Dalton's saw-grass, drowsing in the shade of one of the four old shaggy cottonwood trees which derived their existence from the spring. "Nice animals," he allowed.

McGregor's grin broadened. "We didn't steal them," he said, reading the tough old man's mind. "Don't have the bills of sale with us, though, to prove it."

Charley Durant turned, went back to the pressed-flat saw-grass where he too had been drowsing, and dropped down in silence, going to work fashioning a smoke.

Dalton came still closer, eyed the saddlery, eyed the weapons he could see, then asked a predictable question. "Since there aren't no cow outfits down here, and since you boys are clearly riders, either you never seen this country before and figured there might be work on the desert, or else you are lost."

Durant, lighting his cigarette, shot McGregor an amused look. Mack's amused expression lingered as he replied to old Dalton.

"We could be renegades from up north making a run for the line," he said, but old Dalton shook his head slowly about this.

"Not in my experience, young feller. I've lived down here more years than you are old, and in that time I've seen 'em all, the mean ones, the scairt ones, the hurt ones and the crazy ones. Do you know what they all got in common?"

"No. What?"

Dalton pointed around the camp. "They don't stop to loaf for a day or two, when they're this close. They keep right on going."

Charley's ironic amusement prompted him to speak out, finally. "Sit," he told Dalton. "Care for a smoke?"

The older man did not answer, but he squatted, still leaning on his carbine, and looked Charley Durant up and down, before he eventually said, "Hell! I know. You're a pair of lousy lawmen!"

McGregor laughed. "Not a badge between us," he truthfully retorted. "Is there some reason why we can't just be what I told you; just a couple of fellers passing through?"

Dalton pondered a moment, then either accepted this or decided he was not going to get the truth anyway, and leaned aside his carbine to rummage for his own sack of makings and go to work rolling a cigarette. As he worked, head tipped downward, he said, "You boys been here since yesterday."

It was a statement, not a question. Durant and McGregor exchanged another look. "And with any luck," said Durant, "we'll be pulling out today." He cocked his head at the mid-way sun. "Before noon — with any luck."

Dalton finished shaping his smoke, lighted it, also cocked an eye at the morning sun, and said, "You're waiting for someone."

That was true, but neither of the younger men confirmed it. McGregor changed the subject. "Where are your buildings?"

Dalton gestured indifferently. "North-ward a couple miles, a little farther from the stageroad. Don't have much up there, a four-room mud house, a mud barn, some breaking corrals, but I got some fine big old trees and a fine flow of water." It was the trees and water that mattered in this country. If there had been such a thing as a plantation or a genuine mansion in the south desert countryside, people would have been unimpressed, unless they also had trees and plenty of good water.

Charley Durant settled both shoulders against the pale, smooth bark of a cottonwood, looked over where the road was distantly visible, shimmering in the rising heat, then said, "It's a lonesome land," to old Dalton, who agreed with that.

"Lonesome, and damned awful quiet most of the time. A man could take himself a Mex woman. But hell, at my age what would be the point of that?"

Durant and McGregor looked steadily at their host. Obviously, Dalton did not live down here because he did not want to live anywhere else; the Southwest had its share of old nightriders, old fugitives of one kind or another. Age changed men a lot; some it mellowed, and some it made too infirm in body to still respond to the violent urgings of their thoughts. Dalton, perhaps a violent man once, no longer was; if the law wanted him somewhere, the old posters would be yellowed with age.

Charley had a question: "You bothered much by horse thieves, up here?"

Dalton reacted as though a nerve had been touched. "Horse thieves! All I need is to see a man on my range carrying a rope and heading towards a band of my horses. That's all!"

Charley mildly said, "You *are* bothered

by them," but old Dalton did not hear. "Damned lousy thieves," he bellowed. "If there's one thing in this life I can't abide, it's a damned lousy thief! Yas, I get horse thieves up here. When I saw you boys I thought sure I had another pair of them. Outlaws comin' south on the run, raid me when they can. I've buried a few, but the worst sons of bitches are those Messicans who come raiding up out of Chihuahua, riding wore-out animals, beat down and starved. They've cost me a fortune, over the years."

This tirade was still in progress when Charley lazily raised up and glanced down-country, motionless where he sat next to the tall old cottonwood tree.

The country sloped southward from this water-hole, which was the reason Durant and McGregor had decided to camp here for a day or two. The view was uninter-rupted for miles in all directions, but they were only interested in the southward course, over where the dusty, corpse-grey old stageroad ran as straight as an arrow down to Timorato.

Durant pointed, ignoring old Dalton's furious denunciation. McGregor twisted, stared a long while, then shifted his entire position. There was a solitary rider coming

59

northward, slowly and with extreme caution, the long ears of his big saddle-mule distinctly visible even though the rider tried to keep plenty of scrub brush between himself and the roadway.

Dalton stopped speaking, leaned to stare off southerly in the direction the younger men were peering, and was diverted by a sound which came, softly and distantly at first, then with more authenticity; it was the chain-harness rattle of teams upon a vehicle tongue. Dalton turned, squinted, then said, "Yonder's coming the nine o'clock stage from Las Crucas, right on time; it's almost eleven o'clock."

Durant and McGregor rolled to their feet and only indifferently glanced round to pick up the sound of the stage. They did not see it until roughly ten minutes had passed and the sighting had caught up with the sounds.

Dalton, standing, leaning upon his carbine, began to look slightly worried, slightly suspicious, as that southward mule-back rider turned off and was lost from sight in the thorny old dusty thorn-pin-bush, and mesquite. "That," he announced, "is how a man acts when he's fixin' to stop a stage. He hides his horse first."

Durant and McGregor said nothing.

They waited until the coach was well in sight, then turned back to watch that seemingly empty broad expanse of shimmering southward country.

Eventually, Dalton rammed a stiff arm forward saying, "There! You see him at the side of the road with his Winchester? Sure as hell, he's going to rob the coach." Dalton dropped his arm and whirled. "Get astride," he called. "Hurry it up!"

Durant sprang, hauled the older man back around and held him a moment. "Don't interfere," he commanded.

Dalton stared. "Well, I'll be damned. *That's* who you boys was waiting for. You're lousy highwaymen!"

"No," said Charley, "we're not highwaymen, but we don't want anyone to interfere when that greaser stops the coach." He released old Dalton. "Don't ask a lot of questions, either, just stand still and watch."

The coach seemed to be slackening speed even before it swept past, continuing on down to the area where Alfredo Montenegro had established his ambush. There was no gunguard up beside the driver, and the way the coach was rocking and pitching on slack thoroughbraces indicated that it had either no load at all, or a very light load.

The highwayman sprang forth and old Dalton caught his breath as the Mexican raised his Winchester. At once the distant, high call of the driver hauling his horses down to a halt, rang dully through the heat, back to where Durant and McGregor watched.

The Mexican disarmed the driver then went to the side of the coach. He climbed inside, remained in there a few minutes, climbed back out, ordered the mail-pouch thrown down, then flagged the driver on his way.

"Stole the gawddamned mail," muttered Dalton.

McGregor, waiting until the highwayman had dashed back into the underbrush, turned and without a word grabbed at his bedroll, his coffee pot, and kicked dirt over their dying little fire. He did not say a word. Neither did Charley Durant who also hastened to get ready to ride.

Dalton watched, completely baffled, and when the younger men were astride, old Dalton simply shook his head. It did not make a damned bit of sense to him, any of it. *Now,* they were going after that highwayman, and hell, they could have caught him flat-footed when he was on the ground in the roadway.

Durant and McGregor disappeared southward, loping easily in and out among the bushes. They were not riding fast enough to overtake Alfredo Montenegro, nor had they ever intended to overtake him.

Finally, McGregor laughed, thinking of the look on the old horse-rancher's face, back there at the cottonwood spring. Durant smiled, too, without taking his eyes off the onward country for one moment.

6

A SOURCE OF REVELATIONS

Montenegro turned westerly, riding on roughly the same route he had used on his earlier trip up out of Mexico, but this time he made much better time.

The heat was at its worst when McGregor, wiping off sweat, dourly said, "Handleman didn't have to give him his *best* mule."

They probably could not have overtaken the *bandido* if they had wanted to. Not in an endurance contest anyway; mules were tougher than horses. Not as fast, just a lot tougher. But where they rode now, southwest of Timorato and about parallel to it, speed was not an issue.

Durant pointed to that juniper-hillock he'd squatted on the first day, watching for Montenegro. "Shade but no water," he remarked.

The Mexican did not halt. He rode through the worst of the heat, heading for the border as though he were already tardy for a rendezvous.

Durant saw the little mound of white-painted stones which served as boundary markers where the international line ran, and turned off into a sweltering sandwash to dismount, shake off sweat, then stand at his animal's head watching.

Montenegro did not even hesitate after he was back in the State of Chihuahua, which prompted McGregor to say he felt sorry for the mule. Then he stepped back to lift down the canteen, drink and offer it to Durant, who refused it and continued to watch until Montenegro was lost in among the dancing layers of shimmery haze, down where even the scrub brush diminished, leaving only sandy, shallow, sterile countryside for many miles.

McGregor said, "Well; he got his message and now he's gone to deliver it, and if he doesn't think Handleman was put up to letting him go, that just might end our part in this game of hide and seek."

They eventually rode out of the arroyo, eastward, cutting across the stageroad miles below Timorato in the later afternoon, killing time until it got dark enough to ride northward into the town.

They reached Timorato when only three

65

lights showed. One up at the stage depot, another out front of the liverybarn, and the third light glowing palely from two little barred windows in the jailhouse office of Marshal Corbett.

They went out and around, bypassing the town, and did not stop until they reached the rude *jacal* of a very old Mexican who made a very mean living out of gathering faggots on his old burro. He sold the wood around Timorato where it was used for cooking and, occasionally, along towards the tag-end of each year, for heating, although if he had tried to live on what he made selling heating wood, he would have starved.

They had noticed this *jacal* before. It had two faggot corrals and a dug-well. They rode in out of the darkness, dismounted without a sound, and over where wavering candlelight shone from a small, glassless window in the hut's front wall, they could hear someone muttering a rosary in quavering border-Spanish.

Charley held out a hand for the reins to Mack's horse. Without a word passing between them, Charley then turned towards the one vacant corral while Mack strode over to the hut, gently pushed open the latchless door, and when the old praying *peon* looked through the smoky gloom of his solitary room and saw that armed, thick *gringo* standing in shadows, his face etched evilly in the wavering light, he stopped praying. He also almost stopped breathing. In quiet Spanish McGregor said, "Be tranquil, old man. I mean you no harm. We are two and wish to use your water and your corral for this night. For which there shall be money. It is all right, then?"

The frail old, very dark Mexican still did not move nor speak, so McGregor reached in a pocket, stepped fully inside and placed four silver cartwheels upon the rickety table, and smiled. Ordinarily he would have put a third as much money on the table, and a day later his conscience would pain him over this largesse, but right at the moment all he saw — and felt — was grinding poverty, loneliness, and frail old age.

The old man's rheumy black eyes dropped to the spot where dull silver shone in poor candlelight. Finally, he arose, beads and crucifix dangling from one thin-veined old claw-like hand. In English he said, "You are welcome." There was not even a hint of accent.

McGregor considered the parchment-like old face. In Spanish he said, "Your name is what?"

The old man shuffled to the table and drew himself as erect as he possibly could. Again in English, his answer was reedy, but with a hint of pride, "I am Eusebio Sanchez, *Señor*. I was a soldier in this land almost seventy years ago, serving the King of Spain. I was also the interpreter for General Santa Anna in Texas, after the fall of the Alamo, and our defeat at San Jacinto. I lived for nine years in New York."

McGregor sighed. That other old man, up north, did not live here from choice, and *this* old man did; there was nothing to be said about this. Then Eusebio Sanchez surprised McGregor.

"I have seen you and your companion before, upon the road riding north. When you have lived this long, *Señor*, you will not remember much, but you will never forget how to make judgments of men."

Charley walked up out of the darkness, looked in, crossed the threshold and inclined his head in the direction of Eusebio Sanchez. The old man studied Charley, then turned back to Mack. "You are welcome to my corral and my water." For the first time, he lapsed into border-Spanish.

"My house is your house, *caballeros*." Then he glanced at the silver on the table. "But not for money."

Charley, standing loose and relaxed, eyed those four silver dollars, and slowly raised his eyes to McGregor's face in surprise. McGregor ignored him.

"Take the money," he told the old man, "because, as a friend who respects you, I am too poor to have anything else to leave."

Eusebio Sanchez showed wet gums in a gentle smile of complete understanding. "As you wish. Now, sit at the table. I have goat milk and cheese and a little tequila. A rude supper, but better than no supper at all, eh?"

Charley sat, alternately watching his partner and the old man. When McGregor removed his hat and straddled a smooth-worn old wooden bench, he made a little gesture of resignation towards Durant, then dug out his makings and rolled a cigarette.

Eusebio Sanchez, a man of ancient honors and even yet, a full measure of pride, was not a very good housekeeper, but if the goat's milk was slightly "off" and the cheese had stains of green mold upon it, at least the tequila was an effective antidote. Nothing could live in it.

Sanchez came, finally, with a gourd of water, to sit with his unexpected guests. For a while he simply watched them eat, then he leaned and said, "No one pays any attention to an old *chollo* who scavenges on the desert for wood, with a worthless old mule." His muddy eyes brightened a little in the weak, flickering candlelight. "If you are outlaws, *Señores,* then know that in Timorato you are safe — as long as you have money to buy safety."

Charley looked up. "Who do we buy it from?"

"Who? *Señores,* the law here is a *Tejano pistolero.* Marshal Corbett."

Charley already knew at least that Corbett was for sale. He had not known, however, that the lawman was a gunfighter. *"Pistolero, Señor . . . ?"*

"Yes. He is a very dangerous man. But if you pay, he will keep watch while you rest before making the last ride down to the border. But, *Señores,* you should also know that over the border in Chihuahua, there is bad unrest and much lawlessness. They will shoot you on sight, for your weapons and horses, now. There is a revolution in the making down there." Eusebio Sanchez's thin, bony shoulders rose and fell with fatalism. "A different *pronunciado* each year, *Señores,* but the same war. It goes on and on and on. Why, I no longer have enough interest to understand. But it does go on. I would advise you . . ."

Charley smiled. "We'd appreciate it, *amigo.*"

"Stay out of Timorato. If you must go down into Mexico, go east, over in the direction of El Paso, and make your crossing there, over in the State of Coahuila where at least there is still some order, some respect for the law. Do not try to cross below Timorato. A man named Handleman has spies down there to keep track of all *norteamericanos* who make the trip going or coming."

McGregor's head slowly came up. He joined Charley Durant in staring steadily at the old faggot-gatherer. After a moment McGregor said, "Handleman . . . ?"

"Yes, *Señor.* He is the chief for the stage company in this area. He is also in some way allied with the *pronunciados* in Chihuahua."

McGregor closed his clasp-knife, pocketed it, and pushed the cheese away as he leaned upon the table looking hard at Eusebio Sanchez. "Tell me exactly how you know Handleman is involved with the *pronunciados, Señor.*"

The old man was slow in answering. He

certainly sensed the change in both his guests. Then he began speaking.

"I must go many miles into the desert, these days, for wood. Years ago, I could gather a load in half a day, much closer to town, but others have scoured around until now all the wood close in, is gone. I sometimes go down almost to the border itself. I have met horsemen down there, but who pays attention to an old man with a worthless old burro? I have been told by some of those *vaqueros* that they work for *Señor* Handleman. One man, the grandson of a man I have known since he was born, told me he is paid by *Señor* Handleman to go down into Chihuahua from time to time, bearing messages to the commander of the *pronunciados* at Las Casitas. He also brings back replies to *Señor* Handleman. . . . There is one other thing, *Señores*. I have seen with my own eyes, *Señor* Handleman take men from his corralyard to the border, and waylay fleeing outlaws heading down there from Timorato."

Charley sighed, shot Mack a look, then sadly shook his head at Eusebio Sanchez as though what the old man had just disclosed shook Charley's faith in humanity. "A very nice man, *Señor* Handleman," he said softly, and old Sanchez made a little gesture with his hands as though to indicate that, unpleasant as all this had to be, it was nevertheless true.

McGregor looked out into the quiet velvety night beyond the open door. The town was silent and gloomy, and if those lights still burned out there, McGregor could not see them. He turned back. "About the lawman," he said to their host. "Could he be a friend of the *pronunciados,* too?"

Sanchez replied non-committally. "All I know of him is that he is a very bad man to cross. When he came here a few years back — ten years, I think it was — he arrived in haste, like they all do. But when the man who was marshal at that time, a person by the name of Jake Plummer, rode south one time and never returned, *Señor* Corbett took the job. I have seen him use his gun, and he is far too good with it to have been born that way. *Señores,* that is all I can tell you, except that he and *Señor* Handleman are not very good friends. Maybe he also favors the *pronunciados,* but I don't know that."

McGregor arose. "It's worth something," he said to Durant, so, when Charley also arose, he put another four silver dollars atop the other four, and when Eusebio

Sanchez struggled up to his feet, Charley lay a light hand upon the old man's arm.

"You may have saved someone's life tonight, *viejo*. That's a mighty small sum of money for that. Good night, and *gracias*. We'll be gone by the time you get up in the morning. If you never mention us stopping, neither will we."

They left the old man with his unexpected windfall and strolled out into the warm, starbright night, ambled to the corral where their horses were eating, and leaned there for a while without speaking.

Then Charley said, "That son of a bitch. But why did he let us do it, Mack?"

McGregor's response was short. "Easy. You put up sixty good dollars to help bribe Montenegro out of Corbett's jailhouse, which otherwise he would have had to put up himself." Mack turned, bleakly smiling. "He owes you sixty dollars, Charley."

Durant looked at the position of the moon. The night was still young. He dropped his head and looked at his partner. "He also either told Montenegro who we are, or gave him a message about us to be delivered to the pepperbellies over the line. Mack; Handleman is going to get us killed."

McGregor turned and ran a slow look

74

around among the adobe buildings lying southerly, down where Timorato-proper lay. "If he sleeps at the corralyard we shouldn't have too much trouble," he said. "But if he lives elsewhere, we're going to have to roust him out."

Durant straightened up off the corral. They walked away together, through the deepening hush of night.

7

HANDLEMAN

The doors of the thick-walled old adobe church were open, which they were at any time unless it happened to be raining, an occurrence which happened so rarely on the south desert, people could not recall one rain after another one arrived, and from within that whitewashed rude-walled place, two thick white candles burnt upon either side of a raised, age-darkened wooden altar.

There was no one inside the church, but as McGregor and Durant looked up there, beyond the very wide, few broad stone steps, their attention caught by those candles shedding a strangely eerie light, a greying *mestizo* woman walked down towards them, having just emerged, removing her black head-shawl, keeping her head to the ground as she came onward. McGregor stopped, waited, and when the women finally saw those two sinister silhouettes barring her onward progress, she suddenly pulled back, clutching at the shawl. She was a very handsome woman, tall, and not as heavy as most *mestizo* women were. In the soft starlight it was very simple to imagine how beautiful she had been as a girl.

Charley removed his hat. "We only need a little information," he said in English. "We mean you no harm at all, *Señora*."

The woman still stood poised for flight, her face slightly tilted to catch starshine, the beautiful dark eyes liquid-bright and fearful.

"*Señora*, we are looking for the house of a man named Arch Handleman."

The woman's grip at her throat loosened slightly, but the fear was still in her face, abundantly obvious. "He lives down where he has his stage-company office," the woman replied. "And may he die!"

Those last four words were hurled out. They startled McGregor and Durant. Mack said, "What has he done to you?"

"Enslaved my daughter, is all," exclaimed the handsome woman, with bitterness. "Broken my heart and broken God's commandments, *Señores*, and of course, being his friends you will tell him what I have said, then he can send some of his *chollos*, his *peon* scum to kill me, too." The woman took a fresh grip on her shawl, swung half away and hastened off down the dusty roadway in the bland night.

Charley said, "You know, Mack, I don't see how we misjudged Handleman so completely."

They were walking again, in the direction of the stage-company's corralyard, when Mack replied, "I didn't make any judgment of him. All I wanted from him was a little help. I didn't think much about Handleman one way or the other."

The stage-office was dark. So was the jailhouse, now, but the liverybarn had its night-lantern hoisted in the middle of the earthen runway, and that one light still faintly glowed as they reached the sagging old gate of the corralyard, and stepped inside. If anyone besides the distraught woman had seen them, which was highly improbable, no one could see them now because the corralyard had a five-foot-high mud wall completely enclosing it.

There were several low, rude adobe buildings built along the north wall, and three corrals of faggots contained a number of slumbering horses and mules. It was possible that Arch Handleman slept in the bunkhouse with his hostlers, but not very probable, so they went to the back of the office, tried the door, and when it would not yield, McGregor rapped briefly but loudly upon it.

They had to knock twice more before Handleman, lantern in one hand a sixgun in the other hand, came to release the lock and snarlingly look out. He had the lantern put aside and the sixgun still in his right fist when he recognized his callers, and let go with a great groan, then began to swear with anger and exasperation.

They pushed inside, closed the door, and Charley leaned, smiling into Handleman's face, and swung hard, striking the company's manager's right hand with considerable force. The sixgun sailed across, struck a mud wall, and rattled upon the floor.

Handleman was astounded. He was also suddenly fully awake. He opened his mouth to protest and McGregor took his arm, propelled him to a chair, shoved him roughly into it, then said, "You want to shoot him, Charley, or shall I do it?"

Handleman's square, puffy face showed sallow in the lantern-light. He seemed unable to speak, or at least unable to comprehend what was happening.

Charley drew his Colt, aimed it, and drew back the hammer. "The first lie, and I kill you. No second chances. The first lie . . ."

Mack hooked his thumbs, gazed upon the older, heavier man, then said, "What was in the message you gave Montenegro?"

Slow comprehension broke over Handleman's face. "You stopped him," he said, sounding as though he were explaining something to himself. "You stopped him and found the note. Well, hell, boys, you read it. You know what was in it. But you got to understand something else. I didn't tell them you were still in the country. I only said you were company agents, and had caught Montenegro, and that was why he couldn't return when he was supposed to. I told them . . . you read it . . . I told them I'd figure a way to get you boys out of here. That's all. You read it, so you know —"

"Those men you hire, out there in the corralyard," stated McGregor. "What are they, besides hostlers?"

Handleman hedged. "What do you mean — what are they? I got to have men in the yard. You know that. I got to keep the coaches running and the animals fit. I got to —"

"You're one second away from it," stated Charley, shoving his gun closer. "Just one second."

Handleman showed sweat on his face

and saliva at the corners of his mouth. On the south desert, no one bluffed. "They help me do a little manhunting," said Handleman. "You boys understand that."

McGregor said, "Yeah, we understand that. But the way you do it is a little different. Tell us about it."

"Listen, for Chriz'sake," cried the thickset man, pleading to McGregor. "A man's got to make it down here just about any way that he can."

"*Tell* us!"

Handleman felt for his blue bandanna and out of habit mopped his face and neck. "I got a stack of dodgers in my closet. When I see a new face outside, I look him up, and if he's there, I sometimes go down to the border myself, and sometimes I send my boys."

"For the reward?" asked McGregor, and Handleman squirmed.

"Well, yes."

"What the hell does that mean — well, yes?"

"Well, sometimes," Handleman looked wincingly at the cocked gun inches from his face. "Sometimes, if they got enough cash, they can pay me, and go on over the line down into Messico."

McGregor turned and waited until

Durant had eased off the hammer and holstered his Colt. "Like you said, Charley, Mister Handleman is a nice feller." McGregor turned back. "And when they get down into Mexico — what then?"

"Well, I guess they just keep riding," said Handleman, then saw Charley's right hand moving back towards his holster, so he squirted out the full confession. "I send word to the fellers at Las Casitas, the raiders down there who are now *pronunciados,* and they sort of drift up along the border and . . . catch those fellers, too."

McGregor stood gazing at the seated man for a long time without speaking. Charley Durant stepped to the desk, which was locked, tried the drawers, then growled at Handleman, who furiously dug in his trouser pockets for the little key which he handed over. Charley searched, but did not find what he sought, his money, so he went over to Handleman and shoved out a palm. "Sixty dollars in cash."

Handleman screwed up his face. "You only gave me forty." He sank a hand into one trouser pocket as Charley said, "The other twenty is for inconvenience. But I think I'll kill you anyway. Handleman, you're a first class son of a bitch." Charley counted the money as Handleman put it in his hand, then he shoved it away and said it again. "You stole from the outlaws, you sold them to the Mexes to be robbed and shot down and left lying, and you got a tie-in with the *pronunciados*. You'd ought to be killed."

McGregor had one more thing to add. "And there is a girl, Handleman. Where is she?"

The seated man's shirtfront showed streaks of dark sweat. Once, he looked swiftly towards a corner where a shotgun leaned, but that was as close as he came to resistance, and when Mack leaned and very quietly repeated the question about the girl, Handleman pulled back as far as he could in his chair when he replied, over-whelmed with fear, and justifiably so. On the south desert no one murdered men like Arch Handleman. They could not possibly murder them. Kill them, yes, as often as they encountered them, but it was not at all possible to *murder* such a man, even the law recognized that.

"She's back there." Handleman gestured with a thick arm in the direction from which he had emerged to answer his corralyard door.

McGregor straightened up, looked at his

partner, then walked away, into the dark and dinginess of the living quarters built onto the rear of the office. Charley, left alone with Handleman, leaned and stared and said nothing. Of the two men, McGregor and Durant, Charley seemed the most likely one to perform an execution and Handleman, who had lived many years along the border and was a good judge of men, realized this.

He said, "Listen; what the hell can I do? Money? I'll give you all I got. What else can I do? Leave the country? I give you my word I'll do it first thing in the morning. *Tell* me, for Chriz'sake don't just stand there, tell me what I got to do."

Charley made no attempt to answer, but even if that had been his intention he probably would have been distracted. Suddenly, a girl's high wails erupted in the distant darkness, then there was the sound of heavy leather landing upon flesh. The lashing sounds continued even when the girl's outcries suddenly became wrenching sobs. The leather rose and fell. Charley winced; Mack was a very powerful man, when he swung an arm, it was like moving oak. The sobs were suddenly overridden by a man's deep, terrible voice growling in Spanish, that if he ever heard of this girl coming here again, or even speaking to Handleman, or staying away from her mother's house another night, he would return and do to her what the Apaches did to sluts, he would come and cut her nose off flush with her cheeks.

Then the leather strap rose and fell again, harder each time, until a door was wrenched violently open, then the lashing ended. Someone back there gently closed the door. Moments later Mack came back to the weakly-lighted office with a man's heavy leather garrison-belt in one fist.

Handleman looked from the belt to McGregor's cold expression. "It was *her* idea. I'm telling you the truth. She come to me for some money, and all I said was —"

McGregor swung, hard. The belt sounded like a distant gunshot when it came down across the seated man's shoulders. Handleman half sprang from the chair, McGregor swung his other hand. Handleman and the chair went over backwards together.

Mack tossed aside the belt and rubbed one set of knuckles with the fingers of his opposite hand as he waited for Handleman to squirm around and get back to his feet. Then Mack said, "Charley . . . ?"

Durant straightened off the wall. "Take

the son of a bitch with us, Mack. That's all we can do. Leave him here and he'll stir up those greasers down around Las Casitas, and they'll send some of their gunfighters up here after us. Those'll be bad odds."

McGregor looked at Handleman without any enthusiasm at all. "I'd rather ride with a horse thief," he said, and stepped to the rear doorway. "Handleman, I wondered about you when I saw the animal Montenegro was riding. That was one hell of a good mule." He jerked open the door. "Let's go."

There was no change in the darkness nor in the deep silence of the town as all three of them crossed the yard where the horses were corralled. Charley said, "Handleman, you make one sound to arouse your *chollos* from the bunkhouse, and I'll split your head open. Now, get a horse out of there and rig him out. We don't have all night."

As Handleman entered the corral to catch a horse, Mack leaned and quietly said, "What in the hell can we do with him? I been telling you for three years now, the biggest mistake we could ever make, was have to haul one of them around with us any longer than it takes to deliver him to a jailhouse."

Charley's answer was blunt. "Well; do

you want to hand him over to Corbett? He'll be free within fifteen minutes, on a fast horse heading for the border."

McGregor thought, then suddenly brightened. "The old horse-rancher. Let him keep the bastard until we can get word to the company what he's been up to, and they can send along a U.S. marshal."

Charley did not say whether he liked this idea or not. He simply waited until Handleman caught a horse and returned through the gate.

8

A LONG NIGHT

It was Mack's idea and on that basis Charley thought he should implement it.

As he said, the ride wasn't all that long, and there was no alternative, unless they chose to hand their prisoner over to Marshal Corbett. He also said he did not quite trust himself to deliver Arch Handleman to the horse-rancher, and possibly Mack had a similar feeling because in the end he dourly agreed to take Handleman up there. The last conversation they had was just before Mack rode away with his sweaty and agitated prisoner. He discussed with Durant where they would meet, and Durant suggested that McGregor scout southward on the *east* side of the old stageroad. Charley would be down there somewhere, using his polished steel every hour or so.

Neither of them discussed what they would do down along the border. In the manhunting vocation strategy was most often a waste of time. If a man wanted to find troublesome people all he had to do was gravitate towards the places where there was trouble.

That is what Charley did, but he never again used Montenegro's tracks to get down there. He journeyed east of the road, rather than westerly, and while the coolest part of pre-dawn prevailed, he made excellent time getting down into that lower country-side.

It got chilly before first light. It always did, no matter where a man was. On the south desert this chill did some beneficial things. It kept rattlesnakes, scorpions, as well as those big hairy spiders which were also poisonous, in their dens. It shielded a man from any but face-to-face discovery, and it otherwise protected him from hostility, simply because very rarely did a rider travel at this time of the very early morning.

Charley still had the taste of old Sanchez's spoilt cheese and "turning" goat's milk in his mouth. He tried to kill it by smoking but only partially succeeded. He rode, and pondered, and wondered if, when he was that old, he would also be unwanted and deprived, and so terribly reduced.

He got the same answer every other man

had got since the beginning of time. It amounted to: Probably; *if* a man lived that long, which very few ever did.

The night was his ally and he appreciated that. He expected it to maintain its mantle of dusky, eerie darkness until he found one of those whitewashed cairns, and it did that for him, too.

The border, which signified so much to so many people, was actually nothing but one of those widely-spaced little rude piles of white-painted stones. Otherwise, regardless of which side a man was on when he sat his horse in the hush, it all looked the same.

It *was* all the same, at least until one of the border communities were encountered, then the difference was noticeable. Mainly, in Chihuahua, there was an atmosphere of hopelessness, of grinding, demoralizing poverty. Up in New Mexico, even at Timorato, which was a rude, unhandsome place, the poverty was there, but there was also a degree of independent resourcefulness. But in both places there was also something else. A variety of sectional evil which arose from the want and the deprivation. It was probably the same everywhere, except that on the south desert this evil took the appearance of the land itself.

It was harsh and cruel and unending.

Charley Durant dismounted and walked ahead of his horse over in the direction of the old roadway which, down this far, as a result of so little traffic going over it, was rutted and somewhat overgrown. He paused a time or two to gaze at flourishing little clumps of curing grass, wondering what this country would look like if someone devised a way to flood it often with water. Then he grimaced at himself for daydreaming; a desert was a desert and, like the far side of the moon, was never going to change.

When he passed the road, walking westward, he thought he could hear mouthharp music, but when he halted to intently listen, it was not there. He walked another half mile, and this time, when he thought he heard the music, he did not strain ahead, he instead turned to watch his horse. The animal had his head up, little ears pointing slightly northward. Charley did not need any other confirmation; the horse had keener hearing, and *he* heard it too.

Who that might be, not just awake at this hour but making music, was anyone's guess. It probably was not an outlaw, though. By nature, outlaws in new country were as elusive and silent and wary as wolves.

He swung up across leather for a half mile or so, then reconsidered and swung to earth again. If that man up there playing the mouth-harp happened to hear Durant, as Durant had heard him, it was much easier to empty a saddle than it was to hit a man on foot passing in and out among brush clumps.

Finally, when his horse seemed very interested, Durant secured the beast, took down his carbine, and went the balance of the distance on foot.

The mouth-harpist was talented. He played "Lorena" with such poignancy that Durant was tempted to halt his advance and just listen.

Then the music halted completely, the silence closed down, and although Durant knew approximately where that musician was, he knew now that he would have to do a considerable amount of quartering before he found the camp, and this was not just a very big desert, it was also a very unfamiliar one.

He moved ahead more slowly as time passed, pausing often, and in this fashion stepped soundlessly around a horse-high big thorn-pin bush — and the big seal-brown rump of a horse was less than ten feet in front of him. He knew what the horse would do, at the least sound. He stood like a statue for a full minute, then, reaching backwards, planted down one foot, then the other foot, side-stepped in behind the thorn-pin bush again, and let all his breath out in a tremendous sigh of relief.

He refrained of moving for a long while. The seal-brown rump had prevented him from being able to see ahead, and he'd been too startled to look left and right, but if a man's hobbled horse was this close, reasonably, the man's camp was not very distant.

He crept to the far side of his bush, leaned and looked out, saw nothing, straightened back, and as he came fully erect he backed into the unyielding cold muzzle of a sixgun.

A youthful voice said, "About an hour back I thought I smelt tobacco smoke."

Durant started to turn. The gun was savagely jammed into his kidneys. He flinched and stopped moving.

"Better," said the unseen man. "Ease down the carbine. That's fine. Now don't you even draw a breath." Durant felt his holster being lightened. The gun-pressure eased up a little. "Much better," stated the gunman. "Now you can turn around if you like."

Durant turned slowly. The gunman was slightly shorter, wiry and rawhide-tough appearing. He was also no older than perhaps twenty-one or two, and although his gun looked every bit as deadly as any other drawn, cocked Colt had ever looked, the cowboy himself showed no signs of dissipation, furtive living, or renegade venom. He looked to Charley Durant like exactly what he seemed to be: A foot-loose rangeman, probably a pretty good cowboy and horse-breaker.

"Who are you?" the gunman asked. "What in hell you sneakin' around down here for, this time of night?"

Durant, remembering what both Handleman and Eusebio Sanchez had told him, tried a bluff. "I'm from Timorato. From the corralyard up there, looking along through here for a feller riding a mule. His name's Montenegro. Alfredo Montenegro."

The younger man considered this for a moment or two. "Alfredo Montenegro," he muttered, peering intently at Durant. "Now, what would you be lookin' for him for, mister?"

"I was sent to tell him something."

"Tell him what?"

"Can't say," stated Durant.

The cowboy was not offended. "All right. Then tell me who sent you?"

"Can't do that either."

"Well," stated the cowboy, "if you come from the corralyard up there, mister, you'd just about have to been sent by Arch Handleman."

Durant affected surprise first, then worry.

The cowboy put his head a little to one side making his assessment, then his judgment. His gun-barrel drooped a fraction. "Mister; I happen to work for Arch Handleman too."

Durant acted relieved. It was not all acting, though. He said, "Where's Montenegro?"

"Over the line hours ago, mister. By now I'd say he's two-thirds of the way to Las Casitas."

Durant groaned. "Gawddammit."

The cowboy, gun-barrel drooping a little more, said, "Hell; I saw him pass just a little after midnight. If you was sent down to catch him after that, Arch is getting careless. Unless . . . how's come you to be walking in from the other side of the road, over yonder to the east?"

Durant glibly turned this aside. "Handleman said to follow the road and watch for a greaser riding a big, stout mule."

The cowboy scowled in disgust. "Yeah, but hell, mister, not over *there*. We don't use the east side of the road at all. Got too much open country over there." He holstered his Colt still looking disgusted, and that was when Charley Durant swung.

The cowboy's tipped-back hat sailed off into the night as though it were a crippled great bird. The man's head snapped violently backwards, then dropped forward as his legs sprung loose and he collapsed.

Durant swore and worked the knuckles of his bare right fist until the pain began to atrophy, then he leaned, picked up his guns, gathered in the cowboy's weapon as well, and without even hesitating went around where the sleeping seal-brown gelding was, removed the hobbles and headed the horse up-country with a slap on the rump. Then he quartered until he found the camp. He was not able to fully relax until he'd flung the booted carbine far out into the underbrush, had determined that the cowboy had been in camp by himself, and went back where the unconscious man was still lying flat out and limp.

Then he rolled a smoke, lit it, and squatted beside the big thorn-pin bush, waiting. It took a long time, almost a half hour, before the cowboy made several little wet sounds, pushed half-numb hands through the gritty soil, and tried to push upright. Durant killed his cigarette and lent a hand. Then he continued to squat in silence, and wait.

Eventually, the cowboy, looking unsteadily at a trickle of blood on the back of one hand from his bruised lower lip, raised his head, focused his eyes, and while dazedly studying Durant, explored his swelling jaw and lip with a careful hand.

Charley said, "Handleman ran into a little trouble, too, so don't feel bad."

The cowboy continued to explore the extent of damage for several minutes before he tried to speak, and before he spoke he pushed dirt off his face and his shirtfront, then moved to get more comfortable on the ground.

"Who the hell are you?" he asked.

Durant offered no direct answer. "No friend of yours, *amigo*. Who were you waiting for, down here?"

"Waiting? What makes you think — ?"

"Don't stall," snapped Durant, looking narrowly at his latest captive. "Who — were — you — waiting — for?"

The cowboy fished out a sweat-stiff soiled handkerchief and wiped his mouth with it before answering. "No one special. There's four of us down here, strung out for a couple miles. Arch sent down word yesterday might be a couple of fellers try to cross over and we was to . . ." The cowboy lowered his handkerchief. "You got a partner somewhere around here?"

Durant ignored this question, too. "Who was the last feller you ambushed?"

"Last feller? Well; a week back there was a feller. Arch come down with his corralyard fellers and we caught him."

"Outlaw on the run for Mexico?"

The cowboy nodded very slightly. "Yes."

"And Handleman took his money off him, and let him go, then he sent one of his *chollos* from the corralyard down over the line to let 'em know this outlaw was coming."

The cowboy offered that very slight nod again. "Yeah." Then he became defensive. "Well hell; they got the law against them, don't they? They're outlaws with a price on their heads, damn it all."

Charley arose holding his Winchester,

and with the cowboy's Colt rammed into the front of his waistband. He said, "Yeah, they're outlaws. And what the hell does that make you? Get up on your feet." Charley pointed with the Winchester in the direction he'd left his horse. "Start walking."

The cowboy turned, scooped up his hat on the way, and sullenly plodded along.

Off in the hazy east a pale blue-steel blur was beginning to firm up out where the endless, deadly desert met the sky. Dawn was coming, this night was past — and with any kind of luck, McGregor ought to be arriving sometime before noon, or, at the latest, by mid-afternoon, when it would again be as hot as the clinkers of hell.

9

A LEMON YELLOW SUN

There was danger. There was *always* danger. Durant asked his prisoner where the other three border-watchers were, and the cowboy pointed vaguely westward. "Yonder, strung out to cover all the trails bein' used, up out of Messico."

Nevertheless, Durant herded his prisoner along in front of his horse, riding northward and remaining well east of the roadway. Maybe the cowboy was not lying, and maybe he *was* lying. One thing was certain; if the cowboy could employ any ruse at all to reverse their positions, he would do so. If all Handleman's scavengers were not west of the road, Durant could conceivably bump into one or more of them now that daylight was approaching. Moreover, he did not like the idea of having this damned prisoner; he'd always resented having captives, and finally, by heading back up-country he would eventually encounter McGregor.

He did not use his steel mirror until the sun was well up, because he did not believe McGregor could possibly be far enough southward to pick up the flashes. He did not talk much, either, and this seemed to bother his prisoner about as much as being captured bothered him.

Once, he halted in some thin paloverde shade, looked up and said, "What the hell are doing? If you're a lawman, why aren't we heading straight for Timorato?"

Durant motioned. "Keep walking."

An hour later, when Durant finally halted and called for his captive to find some shade and rest, the cowboy put a skeptical stare upon Charley, and made an observation. "You're no damned lawman. I'll tell you what I figure. You're out to bust Handleman and move in, yourself."

Durant dismounted, loosened the cincha on his saddle so the horse could also rest, then said, "How the hell did you get mixed up with Handleman?"

The cowboy's skeptical gaze did not lessen, but his answer was forthright enough. "You ever try to find work when there wasn't none? I met Handleman in Las Crucas last winter. He made the offer, and I accepted."

"He told you what he was doing?"

The cowboy's eyes wavered for the first time. "Well, not right then, but when I come down here, and he sent me out with his *chollos.* . . . A man'd have to be awful dumb not to figure it out."

Charley rolled a smoke and tossed the tobacco sack over. The cowboy caught it one-handed and went to work as Durant spoke again, quietly. "Have you ever seen the prison in Yuma?" he asked. "They've got more gravestones than prisoners. Ten years in that place is equal to a life sentence anywhere else."

The cowboy lit up, returned the makings, looked into the northward distance a moment, then exhaled smoke and spoke at the same time. "I've heard about it. But you're no lawman."

"Stage company special agent," stated Durant. "We know a lot of deputy U.S. marshals. And in case you don't think you're staring straight at the Yuma prison gates — wait until you're brought up in court opposite Arch Handleman. He'll hand you over to the Yuma authorities in a minute, if he figures it might save his bacon a little. You and all the other damned fools who work for him. . . . How old are you?"

"Twenty-one. What of it?"

"And dead at thirty-one," murmured Durant, fishing in his pocket for the steel mirror. He flashed twice, then replaced the mirror and said, "How good a cowboy are you?"

"Good enough. Been hiring out for six years from Texas to southern Colorado."

"How good a walker are you?"

The cowboy was puzzled. "A walker . . . ?"

Durant, watching the tops of the tallest bushes without heeding his captive, repeated it. "Yeah. How far can you walk on your two feet? You'll never find that brown horse again. He's plumb gone."

The cowboy's expression subtly changed. A thin flicker of hope firmed up in his eyes. "I can walk a hole in the daylight, mister, if I have to."

Durant dropped his eyes. "You'll have to, cowboy, because if my partner finds you, or if that snaky town marshal in Timorato finds you, or if some of Handleman's border-jumping friends find you — you're a goner. You got no weapons, no horse, and you're going to be sweated out and blister-footed come sundown, but you'd better not even rest nor look back, because I'm likely to have a change of heart. . . ." Durant looked back along the tops of the bushes. "If you've got one lick of sense, you'll work at your riding trade and maybe amount to something. If you turn back to this sort of thing, you're going to get killed, one way or another, by a lawman or the jailers at Yuma prison." Durant stepped out a short ways to scan the northern land. "Get moving."

The cowboy sat and stared, and possibly wondered if he was going to be shot in the back for attempting to escape, but in the end he may have decided the risk was worth it, because when Durant eventually turned, the spot where the cowboy had been sitting was empty.

An hour later Durant picked up the flash he had been scanning the brush-tops for, flashed his own signal, got astride and rode up-country until he met Mack. They halted in the boiling sunlight and McGregor said, "Quiet down here, was it?" and when Durant nodded, McGregor pointed. "Must have been. Where did you get that sixgun sticking in your waistband?"

They turned southward with Durant leading the way on an easterly course as he explained about the young cowboy. McGregor stood in his stirrups to look backwards, then settled forward and sounded resigned as he said, "And suppose he don't keep walking; suppose he skulks around behind us, and comes up with a big rock in his hand?"

Durant grinned a little. "No big rocks in this country, Mack." He then changed the topic. "I don't figure we'd ought to try and bag the other three. That's asking a lot, expecting to be lucky three times in a row."

McGregor was willing to forget about the cowboy and consider what lay immediately ahead. "Handleman told me something, up at old Dalton's ranch. He said those Mex insurrectionists, or whatever they are, got gold to send north to the people who are going to sell them weapons. I always thought it worked the other way around; that the funds originated in the U.S."

Durant nodded, slouching along, eyes narrowed against sunblast, missing nothing. "Yeah, so did I." He shot McGregor a look. "Now I'm beginning to form another idea about Handleman, too. If the Mexicans have the gold, and they figure to send it north for the guns. . . ." Durant's wide mouth pulled back in a death's-head smile.

McGregor understood perfectly, because this idea had also come to him, but many hours earlier. "Yeah. Handleman didn't just send his scavengers — including that cowboy you turned loose — down here to watch for fugitives. They're positioned so that they can catch the greasers coming north with that bullion. . . . You know, you got to hand it to Handleman; not everyone can be a full-fledged son of a bitch, can they?"

"He didn't say anything about bushwhacking the bullion crew?"

McGregor looked disgusted. "Of course not."

"What was the old horse-rancher's reaction when you told him who we were and what we wanted him to do?"

McGregor chuckled in recollection. "He uses a Mex kid to ride for him. He'd already sent the kid up to Las Crucas to tell the law up there they had a trio of stage robbers down here, and to send down a posse, fast." McGregor's humor increased. "When I told him who we are, he was embarrassed. But it'll turn out all right."

"Yeah. If that damned posse gets down here in time, and if they don't bypass the horse ranch and come charging down here shooting at us because they figure we're highwaymen."

"Dalton's going up to meet them — with Handleman. Incidentally, he told me he never had trusted Handleman. Never liked Marshal Corbett either."

They crossed the road, picked up Durant's earlier tracks, and as they walked their horses in and out of the thicker brush on the roadway's west side, McGregor studied the boot-tracks. "Husky feller," he said, after a half mile or so. "Young and husky, wasn't he?"

Durant threw a saturnine look over. "Mighty sign-reader," he sarcastically said. "Mack, I've seen you stumble over your own tracks."

McGregor was not offended. He reached for the canteen, drank, held it out, got the usual negative head-wag, and redraped it from his saddlehorn. "I'd hate like hell to stumble onto one of those *chollos* down along here," he muttered, looking ahead with a piercing glance. "Maybe we'd do better to ride back northward a couple of miles and sit it out, up there." Then, as he lifted his hat, he spoke again. "Suppose those greasers aren't supposed to show up for another day or two, with their gold."

Durant answered dryly. "Then why are Handleman's men sitting down there all strung out and ready?"

McGregor made no further comment, but he still thought they should turn northward, and eventually they did, with the scalding sun directly above them; at least the last time either of them squinted up there, it had been directly above them, but they did not raise their eyes very often, it was too painful. It was unnecessary in any case; as long as there was daylight the men would be both watchful and cautious. The daylight would last until about nine o'clock, this time of year, this far south on the desert.

The sunlight was not their primary concern anyway; avoiding detection and staying alive was what they had to concentrate upon now. What Durant thought about, too, was the possibility that Handleman's Mexicans might go in search of that cowboy.

If they did that, they were going to discover that the cowboy and his horse were gone, but that his saddle and bedroll and other meager effects were still there, in the little camp, and that would be enough to spook anyone, let alone men who were already certain to be wary and nervous. He mentioned this to Mack, and the stocky, rusty-haired man was philosophical about it.

"It's done, and that's that. Anyway, if they get spooked and head for Timorato, so much the better. The Mexicans with their bullion'll head right on up where they're supposed to rendezvous with the fellers they're supposed to meet, and if we get lucky as hell, we just might be able to catch the whole blasted corralful of them."

Durant turned this over in his mind a moment before speaking. "Just the two of us? There's going to be an armed escort with those pepperbellies, and sure as hell, up where they deliver that gold, there's going to be another herd of fellers bristling with guns."

McGregor did not deny this. "Maybe the Las Crucas posse'll show up in time," he said, and this remark earned him a long, pained look from his riding partner, as they rode along with the world through which they were passing shimmering and hazy and breathlessly hot.

The sun finally appeared to be slanting away. It was, in fact, well down the westerly heavens, but since there were no shadows, no amelioration of the heat, and no lessening of the glare, it did not seem like afternoon.

The only thing that appeared to bother McGregor was that the Mexicans from up out of Chihuahua might come after nightfall. It was a strong possibility. In the favor of such an idea was the fact that the Mexicans would not be accidentally — or even very deliberately — seen, which certainly must be something they would prefer. In *disfavor* of such a notion, the opportunities for ambush were always better at night, and the Mexicans knew they were to meet *gringos* over the line, so they were entitled to be suspicious. Any time someone was carrying a great sum of money, and there were others who knew of this, knew his route, there was cause for anxiety.

In rebuttal, Durant said, "Did you ever see one of those Mex route-armies? They travel like the Jews coming out of Egypt — all strung out, with scouts in every direction and human hound-dogs sniffing up the countryside as they advance. No one's going to bushwhack 'em."

McGregor scratched his jaw. "No! Then why are Handleman's Mexicans waiting down there?"

Durant thought, then said, "To ambush them. All right; maybe I'm wrong."

McGregor's bushy brows assumed a placid arch as he said, "It has to be a sad day for you, after all these years of always being right."

Durant squinted at the sun, stood in his stirrups to glance far back, then settled forward and pointed. "We got to stop some-where. How about over yonder where those paloverdes stand?"

They rode over there. Beyond the spidery little fragile paloverdes there was an arroyo, a sort of erosion-wash, and to their surprise, the moldy soil at the bottom of it was damp.

McGregor said, "I'll be damned."

Durant just grunted as he swung to the ground, then he looked again, and made his judgment. "Yeah. You probably will be if you think you can scoop out that dirt and raise any water."

He was right; there were always *veins* of moisture on the desert, but an awful lot of people had died of thirst and exasperation, desperately digging for the pool which was not down there.

10

A DISCLOSURE

The heat did not seem to diminish very much although the sun was slanting well away and, finally, there were little patches of thin but welcome shade where McGregor and Durant had a smoke for supper, and spat cotton until Mack thought he heard something, and they mounted up to ride out a short distance, until they could see over the brushtops. By then the shadows were altering the entire south desert. It was becoming a world of illusions; of strange shapes, some real, some a blend of reality and shadow. It was a confusing time of evening, but one thing which remained constant was movement; neither the underbrush nor the shadows moved, but a man jogging on an angling south-westerly course moved, and this made him noticeable above all else.

Charley Durant watched for a while, until the horseman was well in view even though he was roughly a mile distant, then he said, "Just what we don't need, someone heading down where Handleman's ambushers are waiting."

They turned back into the underbrush, rode as far as they dared, then left their horses, took along their carbines, and panted like a pair of worn-down deer as they zigzagged back and forth, making almost no sound, as they reached the line of that horseman. Then they spread out, one to the left of the oncoming man's route, the other one to the right.

The horseman was burned almost as mahogany-colored as Handleman's *chollos*, but he was not a Mexican. His features were thin and hawkish, his mouth was a lipless gash, and anyone who might have seen him up as close as McGregor did, when the horseman veered slightly in Mack's direction, would have recognized that he was not a man to make light of.

McGregor raised his Winchester, cocked it, then stepped from behind a mesquite clump so abruptly that the rider's horse violently shied, and the man's gloved right hand dropped straight down like lightning. Charley stopped the draw from the stranger's far side with a call.

"Don't try it!"

The stranger swung his head, saw Durant too, and controlled his horse, brought it down to a halt, then glowered. "Who the hell do you fellers think you are?" he snarled.

Charley answered, moving in carefully to yank away the horseman's up-ended, forward-slung carbine, then moving around behind the horse to also relieve the stranger of his Colt. "We *know* who we are, mister. What we *don't* know is who you are. Get down off the horse."

The stranger obeyed. He was a lean, sinewy man, obviously desert-bred. He was as old as either Mack or Charley, maybe a little older, but he lacked their depth of calm confidence. He was the kind of a man who never relaxed; probably he had long ago lost the ability to relax. He looked like a gunfighter, a professional killer.

McGregor eased down the hammer of his Winchester and made a thoughtful examination of this latest captive, then he sighed and hoisted the carbine into the crook of one arm, walked up and caught hold of the horse's reins as he said, "Walk, mister. Stay ahead and walk until we tell you to stop."

The hawk-faced man looked stonily at Mack without taking a step. "I got business down here. I got a hunert dollars in my moneybelt. Take that and give me back the horse."

Mack frowned a little. "I said — *walk!*"

They herded the gunfighter over to their moist arroyo and tied his animal there, then Mack went through the saddlebags, and came up with a folded piece of paper wrapped in a clean shirt. He unfolded it, studied it in silence, then turned and held it up for Charley Durant to see. The stranger's picture, head-on, was in the center of the wanted poster. Below the picture was one word in bold black print: WANTED. Below that it said: For Murder, in smaller print, and under those two words was a name: Philip Jutland.

Durant looked from the poster to Philip Jutland. "That's foolish, carrying that thing around with you."

The killer, obviously a taciturn man, said nothing, but the stare he fixed upon Durant and McGregor spoke volumes — all bad.

Mack shoved everything back into Jutland's saddlebags, loosened the cincha on Jutland's horse, then pointed to the ground and said, "Sit down, Phil. We're going to have a talk."

"I'll tell you nothing," snarled the gunfighter, but he moved into the thickening shade and sat down.

Mack leaned his carbine aside, against a paloverde. Charley Durant said, "Mack, cut those tie-strings off his saddle."

The gunfighter looked up, puzzled, but said nothing until Mack drew his clasp-knife and turned towards the outlaw's horse. Then the gunfighter snapped at him. "What the hell do you think you're doing?"

Charley answered quietly. "Didn't you ever see this done before? We knock you over the head, then we spread-eagle you to the paloverdes out in the sunlight, tie you with those strings — and ride off with your horse. The way the Apaches used to do it — they also cut off your eyelids, but we don't do that."

The hawk-faced man looked slowly from Durant to McGregor, then back. "That's a lousy bluff," he snarled.

Mack walked over and cut four thongs, measured them for length and started back in the direction of the seated man. The outlaw turned suddenly, as Charley drew his sixgun and stepped in to swing the barrel overhand. The outlaw twisted to try and spring to his feet. Charley caught him by the shirtfront and wrenched him back around — and cocked the Colt.

The outlaw froze in place. He might

have believed, or *hoped* anyway, that threat was a bluff, but no-one who lived by guns ever believed a cocked Colt was a bluff. He stared at Charley's finger inside the trigger-guard, and very gradually relaxed.

Charley stepped back but did not lower the cocked Colt. "It's up to you. Talk, or get spread-eagled. Well . . . ?"

The gunfighter raised a soiled sleeve to mop sweat off his face. As he lowered the arm he said, "I was on my way to the border to warn some Messicans down there. That's all."

"Warn them about what?" demanded Mack.

The outlaw spat, then put his pale, venomous glance upon McGregor. "It don't concern you boys. Like I said, I'll give you the hunert dollars. . . ."

"Phil," said McGregor, almost amiably. "Take my word for this — it concerns us. Now spit it out, because we don't have forever."

Jutland's narrowed eyes widened perceptively, as a thought flashed into his mind. "You're the law?" he asked, something more suspicious than surprised.

Mack sighed. "Phil, you've got a bad habit. When someone asks you a question, you don't answer it with another question."

117

Mack leaned with the stretched thongs in his two fists, pulled taut. "What were you supposed to warn the Mexicans about?"

Jutland looked from the taut thongs to McGregor's face, then slumped as though in resignation, and spoke. "There's been trouble up — north."

McGregor frowned. "What kind of trouble?"

"The gawddamned Pinkertons come into Las Crucas, with a company of cavalry behind them." Jutland looked at McGregor, then at Durant. "I was supposed to get down here as fast as possible and warn the Messicans at Las Casitas not to come up to the rendezvous outside of Las Crucas."

Durant straightened up, looking thoughtful. "You mean, the Mexicans with the gold to pay for the guns aren't supposed to cross the line, because the people they were going to hand over the gold to, have been caught. Is that it?"

Jutland studied Charley while he said, "Yeah, that's it, and by gawd you *are* the law, aren't you? But what the hell are you doing down *here?*"

Durant answered dryly. "It's a long story, Phil, but a feller named Handleman has set up an ambush for the Lion of

Coahuila's gold-packing partisans, and we would kind of like to bust it up."

Jutland frowned. "Handleman? *Arch* Handleman?"

"Yeah. Arch Handleman."

"But he's the feller who was working with the gun dealers to get some wagons over here at Timorato so's we could transship the damned guns down into Chihuahua in a couple of weeks. He's the feller who said the border below Timorato would be the best place to cross the wagons because it's never patrolled."

Durant smiled. "He is a very clever man, Phil. And you're damned lucky it was us and not him who caught you — and found that wanted poster in your saddlebags — because Handleman also has another little business enterprise; he robs fleeing outlaws in Timorato, or down along the border, then he sends word ahead to the greasers that you're coming — and they kill you and take what's left."

Jutland wiped sweat off his face again, dug out his tobacco sack, silently went to work making a smoke, and when he was finished and had lighted up, he sat there peering out into the cooling desert without saying a word.

The look on his face, though, if it reflected his thoughts even remotely, boded no good for Arch Handleman if they ever met.

Durant went to Jutland's horse, drank from the canteen there, then returned and dropped it beside the gunman, who reached to also drink.

McGregor had been thinking. He now said, "For once, I agree with you — I don't want this one with us tonight." He handed Durant one of the thongs.

Jutland finished drinking, capped his canteen, and did not utter a word as he was lashed at wrists and ankles. Only when his captors were again upright, did he even look at them.

"Any other time I'd hope someone'd shoot your lousy heads off," he said.

McGregor understood. "*This* time you'd better pray they don't, because if anything bad happens to us, no one's going to know you're lying out here. And Phil — just one day is all it takes without water, in that sunlight."

Durant went to his horse, snugged up the cincha, looked down from the saddle at the outlaw, then turned and rode away with McGregor, this time the pair of them traveling southward in the direction of the border. When they were a mile along,

Charley offered his opinion. "That's one man I wouldn't want behind me."

McGregor concurred. "Yeah." Then he said, "If the people who were going to peddle those guns to the Mexicans would hire *him*, and maybe a few more like him, hell Charley, they were in more danger from their own men, once they got the gold, than they'd ever be from anyone else."

Charley yawned, cocked an eye up where the sky was the color of old gunmetal, then said, "How much bounty was on him; did it say on the dodger?"

"Five hundred dollars," replied McGregor, "and it was a *federal* offer."

Charley pursed his lips in a silent whistle. The customary bounty was roughly half that much. With five hundred dollars they could go a long way, if they decided to take a little time off for a couple of months and get off the damned desert for a while.

"You ever been in Montana?" he asked, and McGregor, evidently thinking of something entirely different, looked puzzled.

"No. What's that got to do with those Mexicans and their gold?"

"Nothing. I was just thinking — with

two hundred and fifty dollars each, we could drift up where there's big pine trees, and blue skies, and all kinds of water, and cold beer, and —"

"I've told you before," interrupted McGregor. "That's why you're never going to amount to a damn, Charley. You always want to spend money. You've got to *save*. Never part with a penny you don't have to part with, then, when you're an old man, you'll be taken care of."

Charley said, "You're dead right. Just tell me one thing — why did you give that old faggot-gatherer four silver dollars when he'd have been just as happy with one?"

McGregor blew out his cheeks, scanned the soft-scented southerly distances, and did not answer, did not speak at all until someone off in the far distance, made a wolf's call, then all McGregor said was: "There are no wolves on the south desert. There's nothing bigger than swift-foxes and stunted coyotes."

They rode standing in their stirrups for a short distance, but there was nothing to be made out southward, and that wolf-call was not repeated. As they sat down again, Durant was of the opinion the call had probably been made by Handleman's men in ambush. If it had, it signified something

Durant would have liked to have known about.

"Maybe," he said to McGregor, "they've found that empty camp where I captured the cowboy."

McGregor did not think so. "My guess is that one of them down over the line doing a little scouting, has seen riders heading this way."

They slackened their gait to a slow walk, looking and listening, and bearing slightly more westerly.

11

FUGITIVES!

Gradually, Durant and McGregor became aware of a sound — actually more of a *sensation* — which came into the evening air around them. It was similar to the sound one might hear — or feel — if there were a huge pair of wings beating invisibly not too far away. It was a reverberation more than an actual sound.

They stopped and sat perfectly still trying to guess what it was and from which direction it was coming. It did not seem to increase for a long while, nor did it recede.

Durant swung out of the saddle, sank to his knees and pressed an ear to the ground. When he arose he stared southward, then to the left and right. He did not say a word until he had remounted and picked up the reins.

McGregor prompted him. "A stampede?"

Durant nodded. "Yeah. But there are no cattle down here. I haven't seen a single sign of cattle, even back up there at

124

Dalton's horse ranch."

McGregor was less concerned with the possibility than he was with the danger. If they were in front of it — whatever it was — they could be overrun and ground into small pieces. "From what direction?" he asked, and turned slightly to peer westerly as he asked. Over there, a familiar sound came — someone was riding a horse, fast, out there, and he was heading for the roadway, which was on the left, or to the east, of Durant and McGregor.

Durant heard this horseman too, and made no attempt to reply to the question as he hauled his horse around spurring it towards a thorny thicket.

McGregor, farther from cover, did not have enough time. The horseman was coming fast, too fast for Mack to escape being seen as the rider zigzagged through the underbrush, jumped his horse over a squatty, knee-high thicket he could not avoid ploughing through otherwise, and he was still in the air when he saw McGregor.

Mack had an advantage, he had known the rider was approaching, but the rider was taken completely by surprise as his horse sailed over the bush and came down.

Mack drew and aimed, then yelled, "Hold it!"

The horseman had no difficulty reining up; his horse still had his legs bunched close, to momentarily halt, when he hit the ground. One light touch on the reins and he sat back against his own momentum, spread his legs and stood still, bunched and ready to spring in any direction, but motionless.

The rider was a Mexican, probably one of Handleman's *chollos*. He had a carbine under his right leg and a tied-down pistol with an ivory grip on his right thigh. He was younger than McGregor, but older than that cowboy Durant had captured — then had released.

Right now, the Mexican's expression showed fright even through the surprise when he first saw McGregor, and in spite of the pointed gun. When he hauled back on his reins, he broke off staring at McGregor to look over one shoulder.

Charley Durant eased forward, and the Mexican turned back to stare at both the men in front of him. He said, "Who are you?" But before there could possibly be an answer he blurted out a statement. "If you don't run for it they will kill you." He raised his rein-hand as he said this, and although McGregor lowered his Colt, he told the Mexican not to move. Then he asked who the Mexican was running from.

For a moment the Mexican did not respond, he was listening to that strange reverberation. Then he gestured with an outflung right arm. "They are cutting us off. They are coming in from all around us. *Señores,* if the three of us don't run for it *now,* it will be too late."

McGregor did not budge. "*Who* is trying to surround us?"

The *chollo* answered quickly, putting his head to one side trying to assess the sounds even as he spoke. "It is a company of their cavalry. *Señor* Handleman said it would be only maybe two pack-mules and an armed escort of about ten men. *Caramba!* It is a whole company of them. *Señores; por Dios,* we can't stay here!"

Finally, now, McGregor and Durant could understand those sounds. They were no longer distant, which made it possible to distinguish individual sounds out of the entire increasing noise. Horsemen were indeed sweeping up-country to the west, out where the *chollo* had ridden from.

Mack put up his gun, turned and assessed the sounds to the east of them, over beyond the roadway. He looked at Durant with a puzzled expression. "What in the hell are they *doing?*"

The Mexican answered. "*Señores,* they

had *Indios* coursing ahead on foot. The Indians found us. . . . We were waiting to make an ambush."

Durant did not wait to hear more, he turned his horse directly northward, which seemed the only way they could ride without encountering guerilla horsemen. He called to Mack and the terrified Mexican. "Head out!"

It was an eerie flight. They could *hear* horsemen all around them, but they saw none. McGregor swung close to Durant looking completely baffled. "If they found Handleman's bushwhackers, why didn't we hear any shooting?"

Durant did not try to answer. He did not *have* an answer, and right at this moment he was concentrating on riding.

The Mexican lost his hat, and although he was probably skilled with his guns he seemed too frightened to think of them, or to think of the two men he was riding with, who had to be total strangers to him, unless he'd happened to glimpse them up in Timorato, perhaps at the stage company's corralyard, but whatever his feelings about his companions, when Charley Durant turned to look over where he was keeping pace in their headlong flight, the Mexican did not seem interested in anything except escape.

It was McGregor who veered his horse to the right and gestured for Charley and the Mexican to follow him. They obeyed, and at least in the Mexican's case, he could have had no inkling what McGregor was doing. Even Charley was not too sure until he saw McGregor veer around until he was heading for the spot where they had left the tied gunfighter.

But it was not a humanitarian notion that motivated Mack now. He wanted to reach that sunken arroyo over there with the moist bottom to it. He led Charley and the Mexican unerringly through the gloom, swung down from the saddle as they swept up, called to Charley to take the Mexican down into the arroyo with him, then Mack ran towards the outlaw, who was straining at his bindings, looking around himself in the darkness as the sounds of riders seemed to come closer.

As Mack leaned and whipped out his clasp-knife to slash through the thongs on the gunman's wrist, he shoved his carbine at the astonished outlaw and said, "It's a damned Mex army, or close to it. Don't ask questions, Jutland, just roll down into that arroyo."

There was no time to consider the uniqueness of their situation. Excepting

Durant and McGregor, they were all enemies to some degree towards each other. If there had been time for talk, perhaps the gunfighter and the Mexican might have found some basis to form an alliance against Durant and McGregor, but as they all scrambled down into the moist sunken place, gripping their weapons, a Mexican horseman somewhere to the west of them made a high, keening outcry.

Durant said, "Found our horses," and shouldered around Philip Jutland to look off in the direction of that yell. "He'll bring in the whole lot of them."

Jutland shoved up beside Durant and crouched slightly as he tried to make out movement in the moonless gloom. "It can't be a Mex army up over the line," he said, in protest.

Durant turned. "Ask that feller behind you. He's one of Handleman's bushwhackers, sent down here to waylay the bullion caravan. He said it's a company of their guerilla horsemen, or something like that." Durant caught Jutland's gaze. "There's only two things we got to worry about. One is that there are too damned many of them, and the other thing is that they aren't friendly."

Jutland twisted to put his narrowed stare upon Handleman's *chollo*, but he said nothing, and eventually he turned back to stand there, beside Durant, trying to catch sight of the horsemen they could all hear.

Once, there was a flurry of shouted Spanish as riders seemed to be converging to the west of the arroyo, then, when the four men in their protected place braced for the onrush of horsemen which they were certain would follow the discovery of their riderless horses, from a considerable distance a man's voice keened a high call, twice, louder the second time, and gradually, the braced men in the arroyo heard horsemen turning back, slackening pace and turning off towards the west.

McGregor abruptly moved up and took back his carbine from Jutland. Then he turned on the Mexican, with the carbine. When Durant faced around, the Mexican was facing McGregor as though he would fight, but when he saw the way Durant was also watching him, he loosened and allowed Mack to disarm him. Then the Mexican sank down upon the moist soil and removed his hat to wipe perspiration from his forehead.

Charley, with Phil Jutland watching him, leaned upon the crumbly bank and said, "We're no better off. They've got our horses, and my guess is that the ones who found them over here will come slipping back when they can. They know we can't be far off — on foot."

Jutland was a man whose survival had depended upon hard decisions most of his life. He had been baffled, earlier, by the presence of all those riders out in the night, but now he exhibited no curiosity at all, only a hunted man's instincts for escape. "We sure as hell can't stay here," he exclaimed.

The Mexican looked up. "I told you — they have Indian scouts with them. They will find us no matter what we do."

Jutland had evidently encountered defeatism before, too, because he snarled at the quaking Mexican. "If they find us they'll sure as hell earn it, and even after that, they won't all of 'em walk away." He turned on Charley, who was closest. "It's not like it was broad daylight with the sun up there to cook a man; if we jog in the direction of Timorato. . . . Well; you fellers just going to stand around here?"

Durant looked from the gunman to Mack. "He's partly right, anyway; if they overtake us, which they'll sure do if they come a-horseback, they're going to go back fewer than they came on."

McGregor gestured for the Mexican to get back on his feet. They scrambled up out of the arroyo, stood a moment listening, then started trudging northward without a word being said until they had gone about half a mile, then Jutland held up a hand for silence.

Jutland had good hearing. The others did not detect the sounds until they had been standing still for a moment. Mack sighed and said, "Men pushing through the brush."

He was correct, but it did not sound like horsemen, and this made their Mexican ambusher roll up his eyes in fear. Like all border-country Mexicans, he had a deep and abiding fear of Indians. He reached to tap Mack's arm and held out a hand mutely. McGregor unhesitatingly handed over the gun, then he did the same with Phil Jutland, and they started forward again.

They did not touch the underbrush, not even when it caused a delay to work their way around it rather than through it. Also, they were careful not to allow their weapons to touch anything that would create a sound.

Eventually, Charley Durant spoke quietly to McGregor, saying he would drop back, but would keep Mack in sight. He wanted to see who it was, back there.

Mack nodded, but he seemed not to

think much of the idea. He *knew* who was hunting them, and whether it was guerillas or Mexican Indians, it amounted to the same thing.

Phil Jutland saw Durant dropping back, and watched for a moment, then he turned and pushed ahead with the others. He and McGregor did not turn often, but the Mexican did. The farther they went the Mexican seemed to become more fearful, not less fearful.

Charley had no intention of trying to waylay those manhunters down their backtrail, he simply wanted to get some idea of who they were, and how many of them were stalking the fugitives.

The night was fully settled by this time, but there was no moon, which was a blessing for the fugitives, although eventually there would be moonlight.

The night was warm and under different circumstances it would have been pleasant out. Charley glanced once at the glittering overhead array of stars, to gauge his directions, then did not glance up again. Ahead of him, he could vaguely make out the shadowy shapes of his companions, working back and forth to soundlessly pass through the scrub-brush.

12

A BRUSH WITH DEATH

What intrigued Charley Durant as he lagged back listening and looking, was the fact that of all those horsemen he had heard earlier, there was not a sound, and he had been stopping often to listen for it.

Even granting that the soil was sandy and tended to mute all sounds, there should have been *something.* A large party of armed horsemen made noise; their rein-chains rattled their spurs and bit-crickets and other metal accouterments, rubbed, their horses blew noses or nickered or ploughed through thickets, but there was noise.

Except this time.

Charley looked ahead where his companions were sifting through the underbrush soundlessly, fixed their direction in mind, then sank back into a place of deepest shadows, blending perfectly by remaining completely motionless.

As the moments ran past he had doubts about this tactic, then a pale silhouette stepped past and halted, body leaning, head turned for listening.

What Handleman's *chollo* had said was evidently true, because it was an Indian, but he was attired in a coarse loose-fitting shirt which had once been white, and a pair of matching trousers which had been cut off so that they reached no lower than four or five inches below his knees. He was taller and more rangy in build than an Apache, and his attire was certainly different. He was a Tarahumara, a member of a numerous band of Mexican Indians who were traditional enemies of all Apaches — and all *gringos*.

Durant, satisfied now, concerning the men who were stealthily seeking to overtake the fugitives, would have liked to know how many Tarahumaras there were in the underbrush, but his interest was not sufficient to inspire him to attempt any kind of count. There would certainly be more than four Tarahumaras, and that was all Charley Durant really had to know.

He waited for the Indian to slip back into the underbrush so that Durant could trot ahead and rejoin his companions, but what happened now superseded that possibility.

A second Tarahumara emerged sound-lessly, spoke to the first Indian, then they both gestured up in the direction of McGregor and his fleeing companions. Durant could not understand a word they said even though in the Tarahumara lan-guage convenient Spanish words had been adopted to replace Indian words which were more cumbersome. But no Tarahumara used a recognizable pronunciation.

Durant got uneasy. It did not appear that the conversing bucks were ever going to depart. His uneasiness grew when a third Indian came down-country and hissed at the other two. The Indians had bypassed Durant's hiding place; they were above him northward, between him and McGregor.

The first two Tarahumaras slipped away to join the third one, and for a moment longer Durant stood motionless. He had, he told himself, done a damned fool thing. Now he was alone down here, with the Tarahumaras northward; his chances of easing through and rejoining McGregor were very slight. The Tarahumaras were every bit as knowledgeable as Apaches, it would not be like trying to slip through a band of Mexicans.

He made the effort though. There was

no real alternative. Nor did he wonder about the Mexican horsemen. Wherever they were, probably westward somewhere, they were not his present enemies.

Moving very carefully from bush to bush, and gliding across the intervening openings, he started back up in the direction his companions had taken. There had to be Indians on both sides of him, out through the underbrush, as well as in front of him. What prolonged the interlude before discovery was the fact that they were all moving in the same direction, but it had to happen, and eventually it did happen.

Durant was pausing beside a spidery bush looking from side to side before stepping forth to the next bush, when a wiry Indian carrying an old Winchester with copper wire elaborately wrapped round the stock — which may have been cracked — abruptly came around the bush looking southward. He was less than fifteen feet distant. Durant, expecting something like this, and aware of his peril, had that much advantage over the Tarahumara, who, expecting the *gringos* to be up ahead somewhere, and perhaps looking back because he expected some friend or companion to be back there, stared in black-eyed disbelief one second before Durant launched himself forward, swinging his gunbarrel.

The Indian reacted instinctively, the way those great hairy tarantulas reacted. He sprang sideways in a flash of movement, but not quite far enough, and the gunbarrel caught him a glancing blow, raking across a shoulder and slamming into his jawbone. The Indian emitted a cry and staggered. He tried to raise his carbine, but Durant was too close, he bunted the Winchester aside and felled the Indian with his second chopping strike. The Indian cried out once more, then dropped like a stone.

Westward, someone sang out in unmistakable alarm. Durant could not understand the words but he had no trouble understanding the inflections. He scooped up the Indian's carbine and began firing from hip-high, raking bullets through the underbrush.

When the carbine was empty he dropped it, drew his Colt and furiously discharged it the same way. There had not been a sound before, now, suddenly, the area for miles in all directions reverberated with the sounds of a furious fight.

Durant leapt over the downed Indian and started forward swiftly, shucking out spent casings as he went, plugging in fresh loads from his shellbelt. His idea had been to cause an adequate diversion, southward, which would permit him and his companions up ahead somewhere, to gain time.

The last time he halted to listen, he heard horsemen. They were coming swiftly from out of the night-gloomed western desert. He hurried forward, saw two Indians to the east trotting warily back down where all the gunfire had erupted, waited until they had disappeared, then pushed ahead with still more haste.

The last Tarahumara he saw was coming directly at him with a sixgun belted round his middle and holding a Winchester high in one hand as he ducked back and forth through the mesquite and thorn-pin. He was a large man. Starlight shone off a broad, coffee-colored countenance, with a thick black moustache indicating that this Indian had either Spanish or Mexican blood in him. Durant tried to drop low and evade detection. Undoubtedly he would have succeeded, too, if the trotting buck had not, at the very last moment, swung his head. Durant was close enough to see the man's wide nostrils flare as the Indian came around the west side of Charley's bush. Charley shoved out his carbine, the Indian's sandaled feet struck wood and steel and the hurrying man's momentum did the rest.

As the big Tarahumara stumbled he struggled desperately to twist sideways. He succeeded, and in fact was facing Charley when he fell, but he had no chance to use the carbine.

Charley arose, lunged ahead, kicked at the Winchester and broke it loose from the big Indian's grip, then he palmed his sixgun as the Indian arched forward to get both hands squarely under him to spring up to his feet. Charley caught the Indian over the head and dropped him like a poll-axed steer. He snatched away the Indian's sixgun and slipped around the bush, looking elsewhere, then resumed his on-ward progress, but now there was a sound of horsemen behind him, so he trotted. He no longer used all the protection which was available, either. It would do no good, not with Mexican horsemen pursuing him.

He covered about a half mile before he thought he heard a rider on his left, and dropped flat to roll in around the spiny base of an ancient mesquite. It was not a horseman, it was someone pushing aside brush to look southward. He could only see a blur where the face was, but it did not look dark enough to be another

Tarahumara. He raised the appropriated Indian sixgun and waited, but the man over in the underbrush gradually let the bushes fold closed as he withdrew, then Durant heard the horsemen ranging along behind him searching the underbrush, and ran forward again.

Abruptly, a sinewy, leggy silhouette materialized swinging a carbine two-handed. Durant sucked back with the instantaneous reaction of a man already spring-taut. His barrel grazed his shirt-front, then he saw the man holding the gun. Philip Jutland. He jumped in and wrenched away the gun, hissing at the gunfighter.

"What in the hell do you think you're doing!"

Jutland caught his balance, grabbed back his Winchester and glared. "Me! You damned idiot, we figured they'd killed you back there when that battle started. What in hell did you have to stir them up like that for?"

Charley ignored the gunfighter's indignation. "Where is Mack?"

Jutland turned and without another word led the way easterly and northward at a swift jog. He did not stop nor seem even to look around as he hurried along. It struck Durant that Jutland trotted like an

Indian, bent forward at the shoulders, legs barely moving, feet skimming the top of the ground, weapon carried as a balance. Not many white men knew how Apaches covered ground this way — unless of course, they had spent time among the Apaches.

They reached the roadway, paused, then darted across. Jutland finally slackened pace and twisted to make certain Durant was still back there. He raised his carbine-arm to silently point, then picked up the gait again.

Charley had no difficulty keeping up, but it bothered him to be going eastward, across the road, because McGregor had mentioned several times that the dearth of decent cover over there was a hindrance. McGregor, he felt, would have gone west.

He finally stopped the gunman, ostensibly to blow, and asked where Jutland had last seen McGregor. The outlaw raised his gun again, as an indicator.

"Not very far from where we're standing. When I volunteered to go back and see where you were, he told me to come up this way." Jutland lowered the carbine and looked over Durant's shoulder, listening to those Mexican horsemen on the opposite side of the road. "He figured the greasers'd stay west of the road." Jutland glanced closely at Durant. "You tired?"

Instead of answering Durant pointed. "Get moving."

They did not trot more than about another half mile before McGregor and the hatless Mexican stepped into a moonlighted clearing to welcome them without a word. McGregor shook his head at Durant as though in remonstrance, and led off again.

Finally, they halted beyond a wide clearing where a landswell running east and west fairly well obscured anyone on its north side. The Mexican sank down to rest, leaning upon Mack's carbine and looking away from the others. He was still alive, but this did not seem to impress him. He had decided an hour earlier that they were all going to be massacred, and still believed it.

Durant told them who it had been, trying to stalk them, then he also told them why he had pretended there had been a brush-fight back there — so that Mack and the other two could gain more distance. The last thing he mentioned was the Indians he had put down.

To all this Phil Jutland said, "Yeah; and now you got the damned Mex army on our trail."

"It always *was* on our trail," shot back Durant.

Jutland emphatically shook his head. "The hell it was. They turned off westerly and was riding up-country from far out, when all that gunfire erupted. They were heading for Las Crucas like they was supposed to do. Now, you got 'em scattered all around out through here."

Durant looked at McGregor. Mack said, "He scouted 'em, Charley."

Durant flapped his arms. He had tried to do something worthwhile. It had turned out differently. He turned to tiredly listen to those horsemen scouring the underbrush across the road, and eventually he heard one Mexican sing out in Spanish that he had found a dead Indian.

Durant said, "Dead hell, but he's got a lump on his head. Let's keep moving."

Jutland grabbed their *chollo* by one shoulder and wrenched the man up to his feet, then gave him a violent shove. Jutland had assumed some of the responsibility of leadership, evidently, in Durant's absence. Not that this made any difference; when the Mexicans ultimately found them, there would be no leaders and no followers, there would simply be four men fighting for their lives.

Their *chollo,* younger than any of them, began to weaken. When they trotted he fell far back. When they halted briefly to listen, he sank down and had to be pulled back to his feet. Phil Jutland said nothing about this for a while. Neither did Durant nor McGregor, but the last time the Mexican sank down to rest, Jutland shoved his face close and hissed.

"You son of a bitch, you try and slow us down and I'll cut your throat!"

For another mile this grisly promise motivated the Mexican to keep pace, but it was abundantly clear that he could not keep going much longer.

13

CAUGHT!

McGregor was ahead moving towards a thicket when Durant saw a rider suddenly appear on their left, from the direction of the roadway. He was riding one of those Mex saddles with the dinner-plate saddlehorn, tipped back and slathered with silver. The horse was better than average, too, and in Durant's quick glimpse before he yelled a warning to his companions, he saw the starlight glint evilly from silver inlay upon the upraised steel barrel of the *caballero*'s Winchester.

"Mack!" he yelled, and swung fully to face the oncoming horseman. The Mexican reacted to the closeness of that yell with blinding speed. He was not a very tall man, and he was thick through the body, but he brought that silver-inlaid Winchester down so fast Durant only had one chance to jump before the man fired, scuffing a gout of stinging dirt upward. Whoever the Mexican was, he was certainly no novice with guns. Durant drew, wheeled his body hard sidewards and fired back. The Mexican's horse shied violently at the lancing lash of muzzleblast over where Durant was moving again.

The Mexican horseman wasted no time trying to rein clear nor call for support. This was his fight and he fought it. He levered up the next charge for his Winchester one-handed, by sharply dropping the gun, then yanking it upwards even more sharply. The mechanism worked perfectly. Later, Durant would remember these details, but right then, as the *caballero* fired again, Charley had something different on his mind.

He swung back facing the Mexican and squared up to fire, but from his left, and slightly behind him, someone fired twice, incredibly fast, so fast in fact that it sounded as though the second report were a prolonged continuation of the first gunshot. No one could handle a single-action Colt like that unless he had spent years learning. The Mexican was struck hard by both bullets. The range was close. The first bullet loosened the rider on his saddle, the second slug slammed him backwards against the cantle, then farther, on over it, so that when his horse sprang away again, its rider kept right on going off, over backwards. He described half a complete flip in the air, landed on his head and shoulders, rolled soddenly sidewards, and did not move again.

Durant caught one glimpse of Phil Jutland, then a howl from west of the road made them both break away running.

McGregor was standing in place, trying to look back down where that killing had occurred. The hatless *chollo* was with him, ashen, but with his gun resolutely in his fist, its ivory stock showing pure white in the gloom.

Durant yelled at Mack as he and Jutland ran up. "Cover!"

They scattered a little because there was no really adequate cover. Down where that Mexican had been killed several men cried out, and a louder shout called up all the other guerilla horsemen. Durant understood every word of that command. He turned to look for Jutland. The gunfighter was lying belly-down. He had a silver-inlaid Winchester in his hands and Durant could never afterwards guess how he had managed to retrieve that thing, when they had both fled from the scene of the killing simultaneously. He was destined never to find out, either.

A bull-bass Mexican yelled for the

horsemen to fan out, to form a big horse-shoe and close it from the north. McGregor raised up, saw Durant, and called to him. "I take it back," he sang out. "You still want to go to Montana? I'll go with you."

Durant smiled, settled forward and, with an eye upon Phil Jutland, waited. It was highly unlikely that any of them were going anywhere, except right where they now were.

For a while they could hear the horsemen breaking brush as they established their surround. Once, Jutland lifted his head in Charley Durant's direction to say, "If they get to shooting high, they'll be hitting each other . . . I hope."

Durant did not comment on this either. He wiggled his body into the soft and yielding ground as much as he could, and waited.

Unexpectedly, when it seemed the attack was imminent, a man called forth in one of those unmistakable, whining Texas accents.

"Hey, you fellers. I know who you are, up there. You got just one chance, and that's to quit right now and pitch out your guns."

Durant turned to see if McGregor was listening. Mack was not only listening, he was frowning. He called back, scornfully. "Marshal Corbett — whose side are you on?"

The lawman from Timorato answered. "I know you fellers got Arch Handleman. I also know the Mexicans are going to ride over the top of you the minute I give the word. Whose side? My own. And if you got a lick o' sense you'll do the same — sit it out. Now pitch out them weapons."

Durant saw Jutland gently snugging back that fancy Winchester, saw the gunfighter lower his head gently to the sights, and hardly breathed as he waited for the outlaw to fire. But Jutland was not quite ready. He evidently was making ready for a "sound" shot, which would be aimed at the place where Marshal Corbett's voice was coming from. Durant had always scorned that kind of shooting, but he had respect for Phil Jutland's gunmanship.

A Mexican, evidently impatient with the deliberations, called from over east of where the surrounded men lay, demanding an attack. It was this man, unknown to Durant and McGregor and destined to remain that way, who finally gave the embattled men a glimmer of what lay ahead for them, when he called out in agitated Spanish that the men who had killed their great leader, the Lion of Coahuila, should not be permitted to live one more instant.

Durant dropped his gaze to Jutland. All

Durant could have guessed down there where he had missed that richly outfitted Mexican, and where Jutland had *not* missed, was that the man Jutland had killed was some kind of high officer. It never would have entered his mind that Jutland had killed the foremost *pronunciado*. He would not have expected the leader of the Mexican insurrectionist movement, himself, to be riding north with the bullion escort. But evidently the Lion of Coahuila had been with the escort.

Marshal Corbett called out one more time, sounding both agitated and insistent. "There ain't no way for you boys to walk out of this. Give it up and walk out of there."

"Why?" demanded Mack. "So the Mexes can cut our throats? Come on in and take us, Marshal."

Several agitated Mexicans to the east allowed no more talk; they opened up, and at least one of them was firing a rifle, not a carbine. They could hear the bullets from this longer-barreled weapon sing overhead like hornets.

Jutland got off his sound-shot. Whether he even came close to the Texan or not, was anyone's guess. McGregor and Handleman's *chollo* turned slightly and fired back at those men on their right, the

152

ones who had opened the battle, but Charley Durant, without anything to aim at, lay flat listening to the Mexican guns, fixing in his mind where all those guerillas were, and did not fire a shot until he saw movement down through the sparse underbrush where a Mexican tried to run away in a low crouch. Durant dumped the man and Jutland called back to him.

"Pretty good. Keep it up."

The Mexicans initially aimed too high, but once the foremost among them noticed that the red flashes were coming from low along the ground, they tipped down their gunbarrels. Durant saw little spouts of dirt fly all around Jutland, and marveled that the gunman was not hit. Jutland methodically fired back, but there were no more targets.

What undoubtedly helped the defenders was that there was no adequate cover for the attacking guerillas closer than several hundred yards, which was near the limit for carbine saddle-gun accuracy, and once the *gringos* demonstrated an ability to be uncomfortably grim in their opposition, no Mexicans tried to wiggle ahead to get closer. Another thing which helped was the poor light. Although the stars were bright and there was also a moon up there — only half full — there were brush-shadows, even without the general gloom.

Charley Durant lay waiting. He noticed that the Mexicans were yielding in front, and seemed to be moving to the left and right to press their attack. He wriggled around to face the west, and Phil Jutland did the same, facing the west.

The Mexicans were noisy; they constantly cursed the men they were seeking to kill, and called back and forth among themselves.

Finally, unable to safely or even prudently push in close enough to actually sight in on their enemies, the Mexicans tried an old Indian trick; they brought up a number of horses and sent them charging straight at the *gringos*, then a number of Mexicans sprang up in the wake and dust of these panic-stricken animals, to take best advantage of the cover of horseflesh.

But only one of the defenders was nearly panicked by this ruse. Handleman's Mexican sprang up to avoid the horses, and began firing wildly left and right. McGregor tried to yell over the gunfire for the man to get down. The Mexican probably did not hear him, but in any case he did not heed him. He darted directly across in front of McGregor heading for the big thicket where Durant was lying. He got two-thirds of the way along when his gun went empty.

One of the scuttling guerillas behind the horses dropped to one knee and fired. Handleman's Mexican sucked back, then tried to come on again. Another guerilla fired and this time the injured man fell dead.

Jutland cut down the first of those guerillas, and Durant got the second one. Then those two, supported by McGregor, who was farther back to the right of Phil Jutland, covered their heads while the stampeding horses veered away from the visible stands of brush, and crashed rearward in a dead run. Instantly, Jutland raised up, and very systematically cut down three oncoming, crouched guerillas.

McGregor and Durant had similar targets and kept firing until the Mexicans broke and fled left and right, yelling.

There should have been a respite, but there was none. Durant, with only a vague idea of the number of their attackers, thought there had to be about three times as many Mexicans as he and Jutland and McGregor had bullets. If this were so, regardless of whether they killed more guerillas or not, this fight was only going to end one way.

He called to Jutland. "Don't waste slugs!"

Jutland did not even raise his head when he snarled an answer. "Why not? We're not going out of here!"

Then the respite arrived, when no one expected it. It did not seem that anyone had ordered the guerillas to cease firing. It was one of those spontaneous things which sometimes occurred in a battle; everyone happened to be shifting position, or reloading, or at any rate peering ahead at about the same time, holding back from firing.

The silence was in most ways worse than the fighting. Durant shoved himself back as far as he could beneath his flourishing old bush, and shook clammy perspiration off his face while straining to catch sight of movement in the west.

He was confident the guerillas would be edging closer. There was nothing else for them to do during this lull.

Jutland was reloading. Durant could hear him at it, very methodically levering out spent casings and just as systematically pushing in fresh loads. Jutland spoke without raising his voice.

"Sure could use a drink of water."

It sounded so inappropriate, so downright ridiculous, that Durant swung briefly to stare. Jutland was now wrapping a dirty bandanna around one of his legs above the knee. He had been hit and Durant had had no inkling.

Maybe the Mexicans had taken some losses, but they at least could afford it. The *chollo* was lying out there, dead, Jutland had been hit through one leg, Durant and McGregor, still unscathed, were both getting dangerously low on ammunition.

The firing started again, scattered at first, then more briskly. Durant listened, decided there were more guerillas on his side, to the west, than there were over to the east, on McGregor's side.

He pressed down flat and waited for something to shoot at.

A thin, undersized guerilla appeared unexpectedly through the center of a mesquite clump, parting the thorny branches warily to see out. Jutland fired before Charley Durant had his weapon aimed. The Mexican leapt as though he had been standing upon a steel spring, then dropped forward and hung draped in the bush.

This enraged the Mexicans. They raked the area up where the besieged men were pressing flat, and shouted curses.

14

THE QUESTION OF CAPTIVITY

From a great distance someone fired a sixgun. At first, this made no impression upon all those fiercely fighting men on southward. In fact neither Jutland nor McGregor, or even the attacking Mexicans, seemed to hear it. Durant picked up the sound, probably because he was beginning to hope very hard some kind of a miracle would occur. He cocked his head awaiting a repetition.

It came, but the next time it was more than one sixgun, it sounded like at least a dozen of them, also, they seemed closer than before. This time, too, the Mexicans heard them. At least some of the Mexicans heard them, and began calling enquiringly back and forth with their savage gunfire slackening.

McGregor yelled southward. "The army! It's the army!"

No retort came from the hiding places of

158

the Mexicans, but there was no doubt but that they had heard Mack. All gunfire ceased. Durant, waiting for another salvo from up north, was rewarded with total silence. Whoever was coming did not mean to waste good ammunition when they did not have to. They had sent ahead their message, and that was enough.

Durant, looking around for something to fire at, spoke calmly to Phil Jutland. "Just like in the story-books, the army comes in, bugles sounding and banners waving, at the very last minute."

Jutland lay with his head close to the gunstock of that silver-inlaid carbine ignoring Durant and everything else, but McGregor, who had heard Charley's pronouncement, called over.

"It will be Dalton, the horse-rancher, maybe, and the possemen from Las Crucas."

Durant did not comment. Southward, a man's guttural Spanish rolled out in a clipped, harsh command. Afterwards, although the sound was faint, Durant thought he could distinguish men slapping up over leather. There was nothing he could do if the Mexicans were escaping back in the direction of Chihuahua; he was not even certain he would have done anything if he'd been able to. He'd had all the fighting and thirst and discomfort he needed for a very long while to come.

McGregor caught Durant's attention, making Charley twist to look in the opposite direction. There was nothing to be seen up there, but the oncoming horsemen were making no attempt to conceal their approach.

Nor were they soldiers, although Mack may not have seriously thought they were; he may only have said that to frighten off the Mexicans — in which case he seemed to have succeeded, since there was now no sound coming from several hundred yards southward where the attacking guerillas had been.

Durant cautiously shifted his position, stretched his legs and as the silence down where the Mexicans had been, lengthened, he methodically began to recharge his carbine. He was thirsty, perhaps as an aftermath of the let-down.

McGregor waited until he was sure the oncoming riders were close enough, then called out to them. At once a man yelled back.

"Stay where you are!"

The horsemen loped past, southward, which caused Mack and Charley to look blankly after them, then turn and look perplexedly at one another. There was a fair chance the horsemen could overtake the Mexicans, but if they did they were going to have a fight on their hands, and to McGregor and Durant, it did not seem a necessary thing to do.

Then three riders walked their horses across a moonscape clearing, guns in hand, and halted where they could see the dead *chollo*. One of them said, "You fellers up ahead — stand up."

Something in the voice made Durant's grip on his Winchester tighten. Neither he nor Mack obeyed the command.

A moment later, another voice, not as deep nor menacing, spoke out. "You're safe enough now, fellers. Just stand up so's we can be sure you ain't greasers."

This time, the order sounded more amenable, more reasonable. Durant eyed Mack's place of concealment, saw McGregor squirming clear of the underbrush to arise, and did the same. He stood where, finally, he could see over the brush where those three horsemen were sitting, guns in hand and faces completely shadowed by tugged-down hatbrims.

One of the horsemen gestured with his sixgun. "Drop the carbines and just stand easy, gents." As he said this, the mounted man kneed out his horse in a slow walk forward.

McGregor let his Winchester slide to the ground. So did Durant, thinking to himself that these possemen from Las Crucas certainly took no chances. But he said nothing, not even when the other two armed men urged their horses closer, keeping both the men on the ground under their guns.

Finally, the foremost rider drew rein, looked around, considered the dead *chollo*, raised his head to pick up the sound of his companions riding on southward in pursuit, then he kicked loose his left foot and dropped to the ground, still keeping McGregor and Durant covered as he spoke aside to the other pair of mounted men.

"Go get that feller with the fancy carbine, on his feet."

Durant and McGregor did not watch the other two as they dismounted and trudged around the underbrush to where Phil Jutland was, they instead studied the burly man who had been giving the orders. McGregor finally addressed the man.

"We're special agents for Southwest Stage Company. I'm McGregor, he's Durant."

The burly man accepted this with no show of emotion, or of any particular interest. He gestured again with his Colt. "Shuck those sixguns, gents."

Mack protested. "Damn it, I just told you who we are."

The burly man looked steadily at Mack, and cocked his Colt. McGregor reached across with his left hand, lifted out his weapon and dropped it. Durant was already doing the same when the burly man started to face him.

From beyond the brush one of those other men called back. "This one's dead, Al."

Durant's head came around in shock. He stepped sidewards until he could see around there. The pair of strangers had rolled Phil Jutland onto his back. It was true, he was indeed dead.

One of the strangers picked up the silver-inlaid Winchester and eyed it admiringly. "I never saw anything like this before," he said, walking back to show the gun to the burly man, named Al. As he handed over the gun he said, "It's him all right. It's Jutland."

The burly man took the silvered weapon, looked at it without much actual interest, and handed it back as he said, "These

163

other two'll likely have prices on them, too. See if you can find a couple of horses and we'll go on down-country."

McGregor swore. "Damn it. I told you who we are. We're special agents for —"

"Yeah," growled the burly man. "I know what you told me. I also know something else. Your partner Arch Handleman told us all about how you fellers come down here to help him highjack that Mex bullion." The burly man lifted aside his jacket to disclose a small, shield-shaped badge on his shirtfront. "I'm Al McKinnon from the Pinkerton Agency."

Durant said, "That son of a bitch," and shook his head. "Mister, didn't you talk to the rancher named Dalton?"

Al McKinnon had. "I talked to him, yes, and he told us exactly what you boys told him to tell us — that you'd snagged Handleman and were coming down here to try and catch you some greasers, or something like that. . . . But before I sent Handleman back to Las Crucas with a couple of possemen, he told me a different story."

Durant looked helplessly over at McGregor. Their captor looked from one of them to the other, then holstered his Colt to fish inside his jacket for tobacco

164

and papers. "Don't take it so hard," he told Charley Durant. "If we hadn't come along you'd have got yourselves killed. At least this way, you're still alive. Of course, Yuma Prison isn't paradise, but you might make it. Depends upon how long a stretch you get, over there."

A large body of horsemen was coming up from the direction of the border, and when they hove into view, Durant expected to see that they were soldiers, or at least that there would be soldiers among them, but he was disappointed, they were all hard-bitten, bleak-eyed possemen, every one of them a stranger to Charley and Mack, every one of them a cowman.

They had three Mex horses, including the excellent beast with the silver-slathered *silla caballero*, but they only had one dead man tied belly-down; he was the thin one who had parted the bushes to peer through; the man Jutland had shot, and evidently the last Mexican Jutland had seen.

Some of the men dismounted tiredly and went impassively to pick up Handleman's *chollo* and toss him across one of the captured horses and lash him down. They did the same to Jutland. There was little interest in McGregor and Durant, but the men seemed more interested in their recent chase. They talked about it among themselves. Durant and McGregor heard a big, bearded rangeman tell McKinnon they had glimpsed the fleeing Mexicans, but they had flashed across the border down below one of those whitewashed stone cairns and had not slackened pace. They had, reported this weathered, hard-faced individual, driven four leggy pack-mules ahead of them back down into Chihuahua, and McKinnon said, "The bullion sure as hell. It would have made us look better if we'd been able to latch onto that, too. Oh well, get those dead ones tied on, then let's count noses and get the hell back up out of here. This is bad country after sunup."

McKinnon motioned for McGregor and Durant to stand together, then, eyeing them thoughtfully, he said, "I'll give you boys a chance to prove who you are when we get back up to Timorato. I personally think Handleman might have been telling the truth — for once — but I happen to know he's a liar by nature, and a worthless bastard by profession, so I'll give you the chance." He turned as several more men came in. They had three more saddled horses, two of which belonged to McGregor and Durant, and one which belonged to that dead *chollo*.

McGregor and Durant claimed their animals with the mob of rangeriders looking on, and when McKinnon gave the order to get astride and head back up-country, a shock-headed young rangeman eased up on one side of the prisoners, while that grizzled, hard-faced older cowboy came up on the far side to also ride escort, and neither of them said a word, but they were good listeners when Mack and Charley grumbled back and forth.

Durant, thinking ahead to Timorato, said, "We just ran out of luck, Mack. There's no one up there but Handleman and that louse of a Texas constable who could tell them who we are."

McGregor looped his reins to roll a cigarette as he replied. "Could have been worse, Charley. We could have run out of luck when that mess of Mexicans was shooting at us."

The grizzled rangerider grinned, but he said nothing. The younger one, though, was curious. "Why can't the Texas constable help you?" he asked, and got a wry stare from Durant.

"Because he was with the Mexicans, and when they ran, he sure as hell ran with them."

The cowboy was baffled. "With the

Mexicans? What the hell would he be doing with them?"

Charley had no clear answer. "Damned if I know, but he was down there all right; in fact he called out to us after Jutland killed that feller with the fancy Winchester, to give up or they'd kill us."

The older rider finally turned a skeptical glance upon the pair of unarmed captives. "Likely story," he growled at them. "You better think up a better one before we reach Timorato."

McGregor blew smoke and answered through it. "Mister, for someone who hasn't been around, throughout this mess, you're sure wise."

The grizzled man glared, then went silent and remained that way.

There was a little conversation, but it was desultory and seemed to be confined mostly to whatever spoils the possemen had gleaned, including an ivory-stocked sixgun, that silvered Winchester, and the handsome Mexican saddle which had formerly belonged to the Lion of Coahuila, whose carcass had evidently been carried away by his fleeing partisans, because no one had found it, down there where Jutland had killed him.

The night was well advanced. In fact, it

was getting along towards very early morning. There was a refreshing little chill to the air by the time the slovenly cavalcade of armed men had Timorato in sight.

Durant and McGregor saw two horsemen break clear and lope up in the direction of the town. One of them was recognizable as that Pinkerton detective, Al McKinnon. The other one they did not know.

A horse-faced, lanky man dropped back to pass McKinnon's orders to the hard-faced cowboy who was riding beside McGregor. "Al said for us to drift up as far as the public corrals out back of the liverybarn, and take care of our horses, then wait there."

The hard-faced man scowled. "What's he up to now?"

The long-faced man answered shortly. "We'll do like he says, Curt. I got no idea what he's up to, but so far he's been right about most things."

That ended it. By the time the possemen reached the outskirts of Timorato, they all knew what they were to do.

15

McKINNON'S PLAN

The liveryman had just entered his barn when the dark, rumpled, heavily armed posse rode up out back. He came as far as his alleyway entrance but did not go any further as he peered out there where all those men were dismounting. He saw the lashed-down corpses, and the pair of prisoners, and he started away, heading arrow-straight up his runway towards the front roadway, probably intending to hasten to the jailhouse and carry the alarm that Timorato had just been invaded by an armed band of mean-looking horsemen.

He did not make it. A horseman sitting his animal out front, waiting, raised a gloved hand and pointed. "Right back the way you come, mister. Right on down to the harness-room, and set." The horseman turned to make certain the liveryman obeyed.

Out back, Durant and McGregor hauled

170

off bridles and saddles, led their horses to the trough, and allowed them interval-spaced drinks of the water. Neither of those animals had had a decent drink in a long while, but allowing them to take on a load now would probably produce founder.

They tied the animals to the stringers of a public corral, ignored all the men moving around them, at the trough and elsewhere, to bail up hatsful of water and scrub the salt-sweat off the backs of their animals. At long last, the horses were getting care.

McGregor was hopeful. He said, "Give them time, they'll get things sorted out."

A nearby cowboy sourly said, "Yeah, one way or the other. A bullet or a lynch-rope."

Durant raised his head and met the antagonistic look of the posseman, then Durant went back to sluicing off his animal, and the cowboy made a bad misinterpretation, he thought Durant was afraid to dispute him. He leaned while his tucked-up horse drank at the trough, and with a cigarette dangling from his mouth, he said, "Lyin' in ambush just like damned Apaches, figuring to pick up that Mex gold. You know, for makin' decent folks ride all over creation wearin' down their horses, fellers like you two had ought to be hanged on sight."

McGregor, seeing how Charley was completely ignoring the cowboy, adopted the same policy. It was another mistake. The cowboy, his antagonism deepening, took one booted foot down off the trough and glared. "You sons of bitches, if I had my way, I'd have buried the pair of you down on the desert."

McGregor looked at Charley, who was working on his horse still ignoring the posseman, then Mack turned to look elsewhere, and called to the long-faced man who had seemed in command after McKinnon had ridden ahead, an hour earlier. When the horse-faced man strolled up, Mack jutted with a thumb in the direction of the antagonistic cowboy. "You'd better get that feller away from us," he said.

The long-faced man turned, and scowled. "Gus, leave them alone." He gestured. "Take your horse away and let someone else come to the trough."

The cowboy did not move. "Who the hell do you think you are?" he snarled at the horse-faced man. "You're nothing more than the rest of us, so don't go giving me orders."

Several of the nearby possemen were looking over, and listening. One of them was that hard-faced skeptical, older rider who had made the trip back by riding beside Mack. He called gruffly to the long-faced man. "Leave 'em be. He's got a right to his grudge. All of us have. Except for them two, we wouldn't even have had to stop in this lousy town."

The antagonistic cowboy, named Gus, finding support over where the hard-faced man stood, started forward towards McGregor. The long-faced man reached and gave Gus a hard shove. "We're not going to have any of that," he said.

The antagonistic cowboy spun half around, his right hand moving in a blur. McGregor had known this was going to happen the moment the long-faced man shoved the cowboy. Mack let fly from the vicinity of his belt. His fist crashed into the side of the cowboy's head grinding upwards through his hair. Gus, his gun half drawn, dropped it and buckled over at the knees.

Durant moved. He saw the hard-faced, older man's look of astonishment, when McGregor downed Gus. He also saw that older man start his draw. Durant was less than six feet from the horse-faced rider. He took one step ahead, leaned and yanked clear the sixgun, then aimed it at the hard-faced man with his right hand, while with his left hand he gave the horse-faced man a violent push out of the way.

It was a stand-off. The hard-faced man could not complete his draw without getting shot at, but he had men all around him who were staring straight at Durant and McGregor. If Charley pulled that trigger all hell was going to break loose, and the inevitable losers would be McGregor and Durant.

Charley said, "Take your hand away from it," to the hard-faced man, and was obeyed, but grudgingly. Then he waited a moment, but none of the other possemen were going to make the effort. No one in his right mind would have done that; there was no way under the sun to draw against a man who had a cocked sixgun in his fist.

Durant eased down the hammer, moved over where the horse-faced man stood, dropped the gun back into its holster and turned back to finish sluicing off his horse.

For a moment there was not a movement nor a sound, then a gruff, tough voice spoke from the liverybarn back-alley doorway, as the Pinkerton detective stepped forth, with another posseman, the man who had ridden up ahead of the posse.

As he strolled into the cluttered alleyway

looking angry, Gus stirred on the ground and two men went ahead to hoist him upright and splash water from the trough over his head.

McKinnon stopped squarely in front of that hard-faced, older rider. "Who the hell appointed you a judge?" he demanded.

The hard-faced rangerider, already having been humiliated once, by Charley Durant, did not propose to have that happen again, so he glared back when he answered. "Nobody has to be appointed a judge. Every man here knows exactly what to do with bastards like them two."

McKinnon considered this with thumbs hooked in his shellbelt, his expression smoothing out. "Is that a fact?" he said. "Tell me, then, what should be done with those two fellers?"

"Hanged," exclaimed the older cowboy, glaring harder. "We should have hanged them down on the desert. But no, you got some idea of being a big lawman and carting them around and making something big out of it."

McKinnon looked around. All the other men were watching and listening. Even Durant and McGregor. They did not particularly care about the possemen falling out, but they were not so inexperienced they could imagine what their fate would be if McKinnon were downed and some of the resentful men, like Gus and that hard-faced man, took over.

Then McKinnon said, "Curt, you're nothing but trouble. That's all you been since we rode out of Las Crucas. And you also happen to be a damned fool."

Before the hard-faced man could indignantly respond to this last accusation, McKinnon spoke again.

"Those two fellers just damned well may have been telling the truth about being stage company special agents."

The hard-faced man snorted his derision, but he did not say anything. Neither did Gus, who was able, now, to stand erect without assistance, but Gus's reason was different; he was bathing his injured jaw at the trough oblivious to everything else.

"There's a lame saloonman up at the stage company's office," stated McKinnon. "He's minding things since Handleman's not around any more. He told me he was sure Durant and McGregor *were* company men."

"More damned lies," growled the hard-faced man.

McKinnon said, "Maybe. But the marshal is in his office at the jailhouse, Curt, and I had a talk with him too."

Durant and McGregor stared, but McKinnon ignored them to continue making his strong impression on his troublesome possemen.

"He told me he's been in town all night," stated McKinnon. "Which is a damned lie. You can smell mesquite on him, and he's got horse-lather on his pants." McKinnon stopped speaking. He had made his point, which was simply to set the men to wondering. He turned towards Durant and McGregor. "I told him I had you fellers in custody. He said he'd take you off my hands and lock you up until a circuit-riding judge could get down here to try you. He also said he knew all along you fellers were in cahoots with Handleman, even when you brought in that Mexican who escaped from the jailhouse the very next night." McKinnon slowly turned to face the hard-faced man again. "In case I forgot tell you fellers, that's the same greaser Handleman told me he bribed Marshal Corbett to turn loose."

Finally, Curt threw up his arms. "What in the hell are you trying to say, McKinnon?"

The Pinkerton detective answered quietly. "I'm half of the notion these two prisoners *are* agents for the stage company. And I think I know a way to make sure." He looked back towards the prisoners. "Corbett's coming down here directly to make a positive identification of you fellers. I didn't tell him Handleman said you were in the robbery-attempt with him. I'm just curious to see what kind of an identification Corbett will make."

McGregor sounded more disgusted than irate when he answered. "That's damned stupid. I can tell you what kind of an identification he'll make — with his gun, that's what kind. We know he was with the Mexicans, and right now we're the only fellers left alive on this side of the border who know that. If we're shot trying to escape, or some other damned excuse for a couple of killings, Corbett's going to be safe again."

McKinnon's tough, square-jawed face showed nothing, as it usually did, when he replied to Mack's retort. "Not quite, because you told us he was with the greasers, so now *we* all know this, too. But if you can make him talk about that matter with all of us listening in. . . ."

Mack stared. "You think he's going to admit being down there, with all you fellers standing around? McKinnon, old stone-face there isn't the only damned idiot among you boys."

McKinnon said nothing, he asked for the sixguns taken from Durant and McGregor, and when they were handed over he stood with everyone watching while he unloaded each weapon. Then he handed one gun to McGregor and one to Durant. "You're free. You're free to walk up the road to his jailhouse and walk in on him. Some of us will be out front, some out back. You throw down on him, tell him you escaped, any damned thing you feel like, and you tell him you're going to kill him unless he explains exactly what in hell he was doing down there, and how he got back up here so fast."

Durant stood relaxed gazing at McKinnon. He had not spoken for some time, but now he did, he sounded tired or disgusted or resigned, when he said, "I don't like the odds. I'd just as soon ride on up to Las Crucas with you and face Arch Handleman."

McKinnon remained as inflexible as ever. "Sure you would, but you don't have that choice." He pointed up through the liverybarn. "Get moving!"

The hard-faced rangerider called Curt, growled under his breath, and when the pair of captives, with no clear alternative at all, turned and started up through the barn, Curt stalked along behind them. McKinnon did not call him back. In fact, McKinnon sent three more men with Curt. One of them was that horse-faced rangeman; perhaps McKinnon sent him with the others, and Curt, to make certain Curt did not decide somewhere along the way, to put an end to what probably still seemed to Curt to be a farce.

Then McKinnon detailed two men to remain with the horses, and took the balance of his possemen up the back alley.

McGregor, striding beside Durant, holstered his useless sixgun, glanced back, saw Curt and the others following, and sighed loudly. "And I thought we were being saved at the last minute," he muttered. "If I ever read another story where the cavalry comes charging up at the last minute, I'll shoot holes in it."

The town was deathly quiet. It was not quite four-thirty in the morning, the chill was noticeably pronounced, and except for two lamps burning, one at the jailhouse, one farther up along the same side of the dusty roadway at the stage company's office, there was nothing but weak moonlight and soft starshine to limn the ugly, functional adobe buildings.

As they approached the jailhouse,

Durant drew his empty Colt and said, "If that son of a bitch draws, we're done for," then he crossed the last thirty feet or so, reached for the door-latch, and yanked it hard as he slammed the door inward.

16

BUSHWHACKED!

Marshal Corbett was not at his desk, he was standing near a spread of horns where his hat and shellbelt were draped. He was, in fact, taking down the gunbelt when McGregor and Durant burst in, surprising him so badly that he stood gaping while Durant's momentum carried him completely past the desk to where the Texan was standing. Durant shoved his sixgun hard into the lawman's side, wrenched away the shellbelt and tossed it into a corner. His attack was savage. He half spun Corbett and shoved him towards the back wall, but the marshal was finally beginning to react, he resisted the push and yelled at Durant.

McGregor, back by the open door, said, "You son of a bitch, you tried to kill us down there on the desert."

Corbett turned on Durant with a snarl. "I never tried to get you fellers killed. I told you — when I yelled to you — I told you what to do to save your hides."

Durant holstered his sixgun. "Yeah, you did that for a fact didn't you? Corbett, you knew damned well that the moment we stood up that band of Mexicans was going to riddle us."

"I didn't know no such thing," squawked the Texan. "I was tryin' to keep you fellas from getting —"

"What were you doing down there?" snapped Durant.

The Texan, fully recovered now, turned sly. "Doin' down there?" he retorted, in his whiny accent, "I was tryin' to catch me a passel of border-jumpers. That's what I was —"

"You lousy liar," exclaimed McGregor, still pointing his empty sixgun at the lawman. He cocked the gun.

Corbett, sure he was about to be executed, blurted out his statement. "Wait a minute, you fellers, just give me a minute or two. . . . I knew what Arch Handleman was up to. I knew them greasers was comin' up over the line with their bullion, because I been payin' one of Arch's *chollos* by the month for the past year to keep me informed on everything Arch did or figured to do. So . . . hell, I did what you boys would've done. I rode down there before the greasers got up to the line, and told 'em about the ambush. They had to make that rendezvous up at Las Crucas, they told me, so they didn't call off the trip — they just sent ahead a big band of In'ians to scout out Arch's bushwhackers and cut their throats. They got all but two without a shot bein' fired. They never found a *gringo* ambusher, and that feller who run over and joined you fellers, they never got him neither." Corbett flicked an anxious stare from Durant to McGregor, then took down a fresh breath, and said, "All right; you know the story. I helped handle the arrangements between the Mexes and those gun-runners to meet at Las Crucas, but that's all I done." Corbett paused again, evidently looking for some diminution of the hostility in the faces of the armed men. He tapped his middle. "I got a moneybelt under my shirt. It's got three thousand dollars in it. To earn it all you got to do is walk out of here and never come back." He started to reach inside his shirt. Charley Durant uncorked a flashing, bony fist which connected hard, and the Texan bounced off his back wall and fell forward, face down.

McGregor eased down the hammer of his empty gun, carelessly holstered the thing and stepped to the open doorway.

The first man to walk in out of the gloom was that hard-faced rangeman called Curt. He had a dangling Colt in his right fist as he squinted against the lamplight, gazing at the unconscious town marshal. He said nothing until the other possemen accompanying him pushed into the jailhouse office, then, looking around to ease the Colt into his holster, he grumbled an apology.

"I was wrong about you two fellers. But it sure didn't seem like it for a long while, tonight." He raised his eyes to McGregor, then to Charley Durant. "A man'd have reason to have his doubts, though."

McGregor said nothing until after he had turned a dry look in Durant's direction. Then he spoke, as the horse-faced man shouldered through to look at the downed Texan, and to also disarm him. Mack said, "Curt, we accept your apology . . . but I think it's a waste of time. You're too old to learn patience." Mack, under the hard-faced man's troubled and indignant glare, began loading his empty sixgun and paid no further heed.

There was the sound of other booted and spurred men clumping up the plankwalk from around the side of the building. When McKinnon and the balance of his possemen entered, the little office was full.

McKinnon curtly nodded at McGregor, pushed through to where the town marshal of Timorato had been shoved into his desk chair, and without a word tore at Corbett's shirt. Beneath was the leather money-belt exactly as Corbett had said, and sewn to it was a very small leather holster containing a .41 caliber, under-and-over derringer, one of the most deadly belly-guns ever made, at that kind of distance.

McKinnon palmed the little gun and held it up where Durant could see it, without uttering a word. Durant was not especially impressed. "Why do you think I belted him; that's not the first belly-gun holstered in a money-belt I've ever seen. The minute he reached inside his shirt, I hit him."

Durant did as Mack was doing, he pulled loads from the loops of his shellbelt and reloaded his Colt. Finally, with McKinnon standing beside the desk with Corbett's weapons and money-belt lying there, Durant said, "You satisfied?"

McKinnon answered briskly. "Yeah. To be truthful, I never really doubted you boys. It was just that I had to make plumb certain."

The horse-faced man was grinning, and McGregor knew why; maybe McKinnon had never doubted, but if he hadn't, then he certainly had proved himself to be a consummate actor. He had talked and acted, and had even looked, as though he *had* doubted.

Mack grinned back, and the horse-faced posseman turned on Curt to say, "We didn't come out so good." Not many of the crowding-up men knew what that meant, but the hard-faced man knew, and glowered.

"We got this one, ain't we, and he's bound to be worth something — somewhere."

Durant stepped over beside Mack and jerked his head. From here on, it was all the responsibility of the Pinkerton man. They would put a claim to the bounty on Jutland, even though they had not killed him, and beyond that the affair would be wound down by the U.S. marshals, the Pinkertons, and anyone else in high authority who might be sufficiently involved. McGregor and Durant had followed the instructions of the company. In fact, they had accomplished more than the company had asked of them.

Outside, in the paling chill, Mack pulled down a big breath and exhaled it. He stood with Durant upon the edge of the plankwalk, beginning to feel like a free human being again — and without any warning, just as they started to step away, to turn down in the direction of the liverybarn to look in on their animals, three guns erupted.

Two bullets tore loose great chunks of adobe in the jailhouse wall behind them. One bullet lifted Mack's hat at the crown and sent it sailing like a frightened bird.

Durant saw the muzzleblasts. He drew and fired as he was dropping, picking the middle gunblast to bracket with two very fast thumb-shots, then he drilled the third shot directly between those other two — and a man shot forward around the edge of a southward building upon the opposite side of the road, and rolled into the roadway.

McGregor drew and fired into the center of the orange flash of the weapon north-ward of the man Durant bracketed. Mack did not attempt to demonstrate the incredible speed and accuracy of his partner, he knelt and, as cold as ice, methodically fired. He was also very fast at the draw, but Mack had always been a man who believed in deliberate accuracy.

Inside the jailhouse men shouted in astonishment and tumbled forth into the roadway, scattering in all directions, guns up and ready.

Mack waited, after drilling a shot straight into the center of that gunblast, then suddenly sprang to his feet and went charging bull-like directly towards that building-edge where those three bushwhackers had made their attempt. Behind him, the hard-faced posseman named Curt roared defiance and broke out into a bowlegged run, too.

The last man to move was Charley Durant. He got to his feet after the initial excitement had passed, and while most of the possemen were rushing in a frontal attack upon the place of concealment of those ambushers, McKinnon came up and said, "Who the hell *was* that?" and Durant, standing in shadows beneath the jailhouse overhang, pointed to where his victim lay face up in the starlight. "I can see the Chihuahua spurs from here. Go look for yourself."

But McKinnon remained where he was, his attention caught by four of his possemen returning up the southward roadway punching along a shorter, thicker, much darker man, ahead of them.

"Gawddamn Mexes," he exclaimed, showed marked surprise in contrast to the way Charley Durant was standing, gazing down at that third ambusher being shoved inelegantly along by the men who had captured him. Charley had already figured out the reason for that murderous attack upon him and his partner.

When the possemen came up and shoved their sweaty, shaking Mexican forward, one of them held up a Colt and addressed McKinnon in a voice full of awe.

"I never before in my whole blasted life seen a Colt forty-five do *this* before."

Durant leaned to look as McKinnon accepted the gun and examined it. Somehow, in what must have been a pure fluke, when the firing pin had fallen, it had driven through the detonator-plug in the cartridge case, completely through the metal, and had not fired the bullet. In fact, when McKinnon tried to draw back the hammer, he could not budge it. He handed the gun to Durant, who looked briefly, then turned to gaze at the sweating Mexican. "Who are you?" he demanded. "Why did you try to kill my partner and me?"

The Mexican raised his hands, palms upright in supplication. He was not a very old man, but he looked old now, in the sickly pre-dawn glow, with a layer of jailhouse lamplight mixing with the grey light.

"*Señor*, we were told to find the two men who killed the Lion of Coahuila, and do the same to them. *Señor*, we rode up from the border to find you and —"

"My partner and I didn't kill that Mex on the fancy saddle with the silvered Winchester," exclaimed Durant. "That was done by a man named Jutland. He was killed during the brush-fight down there." Durant handed the jammed Colt to McKinnon and fully faced the captive. "Who sent you?"

"Colonel Fuentes, *Señor*, commandant of the bullion escort. He would pay us five hundred pesos each, for killing you."

McGregor, returning from across the road where he and his companions had dragged the second dead Mexican into the roadway and had left him lying there to walk over and see what was taking place in front of the jailhouse, came on up and put a malevolent glare upon the surviving assassin. The Mexican winced and would not look at Mack again as he continued to speak.

"The *gringo Tejano*, *Señor*, he told us it was you — and that man — who killed the Lion of Coahuila."

McKinnon scowled. "What *gringo Tejano*?"

Durant answered for the Mexican.

"Corbett. He was the only *gringo* Texan among them. He would have been the only man with the Mexicans who knew who McGregor and I were. He could have described us to them." Durant studied the frightened Mexican with thoughtful indifference, then he said, "Where did you fellers leave your horses?" and when the Mexican raised an arm pointing southward, out into the desert, Durant said, "Go on back. Tell your *commandante* whatever in hell you want to tell him, but *amigo,* the next time I recognize you, I'm going to kill you on sight."

McKinnon started to protest, so did several of his indignant possemen. McGregor took Durant's side with a growling comment. "What the hell are you fellers squawking about? They shot at *us,* not you."

Surprisingly, the hard-faced rangerider called Curt, joined the horse-faced man and Mack in arguing in favor of the Mexican's release, and in the end McKinnon, who already had more than enough to worry about, threw up his arms, turned and walked back into the jailhouse.

Durant leaned, tapped the sweating Mexican's chest, and said in Spanish, "Remember, cowboy, the next time you

192

come up over the line, and I see you, you shall die. Now go — and tell whatever lie you must."

The Mexican turned, then looked back as though expecting the customary Mexican shot in the back as he hastened away. Not a gun showed. He faced resolutely forward, walking very fast, and just before he disappeared from sight, he broke over into a run.

Durant looked across the road where someone had just lighted a lamp in the café. It was much too early for Timorato to be awakening, but that wild burst of gunfire moments earlier had probably expedited the awakening process.

Durant jutted his jaw. Mack understood. They left the silent possemen and strolled over to bang upon the café door.

17

HEADING NORTH

The meat was tough enough to have come from a mule — which was an excellent possibility — the coffee was as acidy as the etching fluid used by gunmakers, and when they finally got finished eating and sat back to roll smokes and relax, the caféman came padding up to unctuously smile and lean down to ask if they knew what had happened in the roadway a short while ago.

He got in reply two steady, unsmiling stares and not a word. Uncomfortably, he hauled upright, turned and padded back behind the hanging blanket to his kitchen, and Charley said, "Our pay is due from El Paso."

Mack considered the deadly half cup of coffee in front of him, and spoke as he decided against drinking the liquid. "Yeah. And we've got to write the letter to claim the reward on Jutland." He dropped grey ash into the coffee. "Seems to me the damned company owes us something for riding our tailbones raw, and nearly getting killed. Some sort of bonus."

Durant sighed. "The fact that you're right isn't going to influence the company. Did you know that?"

McGregor did, in fact, know it. "Well then, I figure we deserve at least a holiday with pay."

Durant turned his steady stare. "Did you get bumped in the head last night?"

McGregor gave that up, too. "All right. Then we take a trip *without* pay."

"Where?"

Mack frowned. "What do you mean — where? You're the one who started that talk about Montana."

Charley's slaty gaze got a hint of humor in it. "Can you spare the money, Mack? It'll likely cost us maybe fifteen dollars in horseshoes and coffee and flour, before we get up there. Montana's one hell of a long ways from —"

"I know where Montana is, damn it," snapped McGregor.

"What about the expense, then?"

McGregor shifted position on the bench before replying. "Maybe we could put in a day or two at some of the cow outfits along the way, and get to use their shoeing equipment."

Durant's humor increased. "What about the cost of flour and coffee?"

"Well," explained McGregor, "maybe we could work in a store along the way. Ride into some town up north and —"

"I'm not going to work in a store," stated Charley Durant, and kept looking at his partner. "Mack; how much money you got on you, right now?"

McGregor puffed out his cheeks. "That's a man's personal business. You'd ought to know better than to even ask such a question."

Durant was unaffected by his partner's indignation. He reached into a trouser pocket for a silver cartwheel, and held it up for McGregor to see. "I'll flip it, and you call it, and the loser pays for the coffee and flour."

Mack reddened a little, and leaned to closely inspect the silver dollar as he muttered something about having seen cartwheels with the eagle on *both* sides, then he hauled back and said, "Tails."

The coin fell and rattled, rolled to a stop and showed "heads", which indicated that Mack had lost. Durant arose, picked up his coin, and pocketed it as the caféman came shuffling over to be paid for their meal. Durant slapped his partner on the shoulder and turned to walk out the door.

The sun was up, finally, people were milling over in front of the jailhouse, and elsewhere throughout Timorato clusters of residents, both *gringo* and beaner, were huddling in swift-talking little groups.

No one heeded the pair of men who argued as they strode down in the direction of the liverybarn. Mack was incensed at having been duped into paying for Durant's breakfast. It was bad enough having lost the gamble as to who was to buy their flour and coffee on the long ride northward.

When they entered the liverybarn the lame saloonman, Bob Grant, was supervising the disposition of the effects of Phil Jutland, and turned to stare with candid curiosity at the pair of stage company special agents. He told them who he was, and asked if they had informed the company's office over in El Paso that Handleman was no longer at the Timorato office.

Durant spoke aside to the liveryman, asking him to fetch along their horses, then he looked at the saloonman with an expression of annoyance. "The smoke's hardly settled," he told Grant. "That's not our job, anyway." As Mack strode over to claim his animal from the liveryman,

197

Charley also said, "Mister Grant, you better write the company, and seems to me, if you've been minding things since Handleman's been gone, you might as well go right on doing it, until the company can send in a new man." He smiled and walked away, leaving the saloonman looking after him.

They rigged out, swung astride, paid the liveryman, and when he would have started a conversation, they rode out the back way, into the alley, and passed up through Timorato without even looking back.

The morning was warming up. Mack thought they should lie over until evening at Dalton's horse ranch, but Durant was for pressing along without any halts until they got far enough north to find some decent tree-shade.

They did not do this, though. They did not stop at the horse ranch, but they *did* stop about six or seven miles north of there, where an abandoned old roofless adobe house stood, clearly the victim of a fierce Apache raid many years earlier, and because there was water handy, they sluiced off their horses, turned them loose to graze, then they draped their clothing from a cottonwood branch and took turns pouring cool water over each other from a broken old wooden bucket they found amid the scattered debris.

Finally, when evening came, and the heat lessened a little, they had a can of sardines each for supper, then lay back to watch the stars fill in and firm up. Durant, his eye upon an approaching centipede, said that when he got to Montana he was going to find the biggest pine tree around, which was near a full-flowing creek of snow-water, with plenty of grass around for his horse, and set up camp and do nothing but fish and lie around. Then he brought his boot hard down upon the centipede, and looked over at Mack.

"How about you?"

McGregor was sitting with his back to a cottonwood when he replied. "Maybe I'll find a wife," he said, and did not see the startled look on Durant's face. "A man had ought to settle in and send down roots, Charley."

Durant did not speak. He got over the shock, rolled up onto his side and got comfortable. There were several things he had not got enough of lately, and one of them was sleep.

Mack, glancing over said, "You going to sleep already?"

Durant's reply was muffled. "Yeah."

"Goodnight, then."

Instead of answering the traditional way, Durant said, "Mack, you're crazy." Then he heaved a big sigh, and closed his eyes for the night.

DATE DUE

262